MOLLY

MOLLY

A NOVEL

KEVIN HONOLD

AUTUMN
HOUSE PRESS

"Autumn House Press" and "Autumn House" are registered trademarks owned by Autumn House Press, a nonprofit corporation whose mission is the publication and promotion of poetry and other fine literature.

 Autumn House Press receives state arts funding support through a grant from the Pennsylvania Council on the Arts, a state agency funded by the Commonwealth of Pennsylvania, and the National Endowment for the Arts, a federal agency.

ISBN: 978-1-63-768002-5
Library of Congress Control Number: 2021939700

Book & cover design by Joel W. Coggins

All Autumn House books are printed on acid-free paper and meet the international standards of permanent books intended for purchase by libraries.

The only lasting truth
is Change.

—OCTAVIA E. BUTLER

MOLLY

1

I DON'T KNOW WHERE IT BEGAN OR WHERE IT ENDED, THAT
road running through the desert. No one drives it anymore. The free-
way cut through that part of the state and made the road redundant,
whereupon it dried up, so to speak, like an oxbow lake. It exists now
only in patches and brief stretches, a shallow sunken lane pocked with
asphalt as a Roman road is with cobbles. A satellite image would probably reveal its course, the way archaeologists these days plot ancient
caravan routes in Turkmenistan.

There were towns along that road, and they mostly shared its fate.
Staked and garroted by the new limited-access highways, they died
too. One of those towns was named Santa Juana de Arco. Today, it's a
way station for falcons and foxes. Blown sand lies in carpets across the
doorless thresholds of deserted houses and shops. A great horned owl
has made a home in the roof timbers of the old church, and for her it's
a fit dwelling, because she too is slowly vanishing from the earth, and
it's true that desolation finds solace in itself. A few careless pack rats
will keep the owl's body and soul together until the day arrives that
finds her missing from her listening post.

I wonder if she is aware that, every year, the counters of birds (sad
vocation!) find fewer and fewer of her kind left alive in this world.

What a foolish thought.

That bird knows more of our demise than we do of hers. By the time you catch sight of her, she will have numbered the hairs on your head.

⬛

Who has entered the treasures of the snow or the treasures of the hail? God asks Job in his trials. And who divides the spouts for the rains, to make it rain on the earth where no man is, and in the wilderness where there is no man?

And what of the clouds, I'd like to know, in that wilderness where no man is?

When I imagine the clouds above abandoned Santa Juana, I imagine the sort of clouds that linger on late summer days, when autumn is only an intrigue of birds in the leaves, or the rumor of a breeze in a narrow lane. Look west after the sun is down: the clouds appear lambent as lamp brass, smoke-stained and distant-seeming, and they remain there long after the first stars appear. Only then do they dry up, turning to cinders as the night rises.

But it's only an illusion—an ordinary wish projected onto the sky. Clouds abide for nobody.

They inhabit two worlds; they keep a shadow like one foot on the ground. From their coign of vantage, they gesture over our known horizons, or they bear witness to changefulness without issue, or to some order of existence that might persist, if only in some simpler form.

There's a story that has haunted me for many years. I read it when I lived in that town, and it goes like this. The lives of the departed are transformed into clouds, whose fate it is to be ever returning to their old lives, casting shadows on the places and the people they once knew. If they lived well and were loved, they return with refreshing shade and life-giving rains. If they suffered pain in life, they return with lightning or hail, or storms that wash the seeds away.

Who hasn't sat alone on a windy hillside or a park bench and watched them traveling by, bound to some purpose hidden in their hearts, like ones with something on their minds? The way they appear, *out of the blue* as they say, in a forgotten corner of the sky? Changing under our eyes, preoccupied with god-knows-what, here and gone— not unlike certain people we know. This explains the clouds' various dispositions: pacific, sullen, hostile. Melancholic, glad. Turbulent, rolling, or shouting somebody's name.

That story has become my dearest possession in this life, and I recall it every time I step outside and look up, an act as habitual as tying my shoes. I've learned to scan the skies for visitors from those years. My little greetings do not detain them, and rightly so.

That story, I should say, had its source here, among a people who inhabited this desert for thousands of years. They lived in a place where survival was measured in millimeters of moisture. They must have thought a lot about clouds.

                      ☁

If you went to Santa Juana today, you'd find the brick shells of buildings lining a tic-tac-toe grid of pitted lanes. The commonest trace of departed people, it seems, is their trash, and so it is in this place. Look into any empty building, see the floor covered with dismembered chairs, a cast-iron sink, busted concrete.

A blanket, a rusted bedspring, a red plastic bucket with a caved bottom.

Broken ceramic cups the color of old teeth.

In the middle of town is the church made of wood, La Anunciación, and in the church steeple there is an iron bell the size of a Christmas tree. This is surprising, because iron, as everyone knows, always fetches a few pennies a pound. The scrapyards pay cash, have always paid cash, and will continue to pay cash for iron for as long as civilization endures, and I wonder why some resourceful so-and-so hasn't made off with that bell by now.

Back when bells had tongues and spoke—back when the only sound that mattered or traveled was theirs—people used to name them after beloved saints, like Amphibalus or Aloysius. Or after beloved heroines, like Isolde or Guinevere (who were in those days not wholly imaginary for being fictional). Merrygo was a good name, and Carolina. A martial name might suit, such as Culverin, or Bombus. Mule-bray, too, and Tabor. The authority of the bells was a vast authority, dependable and loved. When the bells called, people came. When they fell silent, people worried.

The dusty old bell in Anunciación's steeple, having forgotten its name, now keeps its own counsel. These days, the rare visitor to Santa Juana de Arco, whoever they are—some misguided traveler, or one of those HOBs, "homeless on bicycle," who range this country in ever-increasing numbers—would probably not be equipped for the task of converting iron into money. In any case, by dint of being here at all, it's likely that our suppositious wanderer has a business sense to match his sense of direction. But I wouldn't think the less of him for being derelict in money matters. I would wish him safe journeys.

On Anunciación's facade, in the manner of Mexican country churches, is a chipped and fading fresco stretching from eave to eave: Gabriel bowing at Mary's bedside, sharing the awful news. Ages from now, a visitor from a godless planet will puzzle awhile on that image, wondering at the nature of commerce within the walls. I suspect they would neither know nor care that the old faith—like the old fresco, like all warm-blooded foolishness—had long since faded from this world.

           🐝

Pass on, wanderer, lest you stir up the bees.

That admonition was chiseled on the tomb of an old Greek thinker, I forget who, the one too tangled in his sums to notice the soldier, sword in hand, standing right behind him—some blockheaded Spartan tasked with destroying everything he didn't understand.

Pass on, stranger. There's no one here.

In Santa Juana today, the absence of people registers as a slight tension in the back of the neck. There is a dis-ease like a weak current, in abandoned towns like these, and there are quite a few of them in the high desert that stretches from the Jemez to the Mojave.

Shadows constitute half of what remains to be seen. In the old books, sojourners in the underworld often remark the fact that the citizens of the afterlife cast no shadows. In the underworld, the dead stroll arm in arm along the gloomy thoroughfares, or throw dice in alleys, or storm castles, or dream up rhymes beside the dry fountains. Whatever their favorite pastime had been on earth, that's what they do down there, but with this difference: they do it without joy or conviction. Down there, they merely go through the motions. Even worse, right in the middle of a thought or a song, they often forget themselves altogether—who they are, where from, what about—because forgetfulness is in the dreadful nature of death, as the oblivious river of myth attests.

We exist purely by rote, it seems, in the next world. And when you visit that world at last, you'll recollect the nickel under your tongue, placed there by a thoughtful hangman. With this you must pay the canoe driver to paddle you across the gray face of the waters. Drifting mists will part to reveal, on the far shore, crowds of ghosts who will open their mouths to protest your intrusion. Have no fear: their mouths will emit only a weak piping sound, like a kettle on a boil, and in a moment they'll forget you, forget themselves, and even forget the reasons why they find outsiders so damn distressing.

We'll meet again on that very shore, you and I, among the bewildered uncountable faces. I wonder if we'll recognize one another.

My point is this. All the old chronicles agree that the dead cast no shadows, although it should be noted that no one has reported back since Saint Patrick walked out of the red lake with his head full of nightmares. No one appreciated what he had to say.

Here in Santa Juana are shades in profusion. Now, in late afternoon, the shadow-tide of evening creeps across the desert to flood the empty houses of the town, to spill across the lanes and climb the cracked plaster facades.

On one wall there is this graffiti: THE MACHINE HAS STOPPED. The red spray-painted words stand forth, blood-bright, in the golden sundown light.

The machine has stopped.

The words might admirably serve as an epitaph or the title of an Irish play. Now why did someone bother to write that?

           ⚬

Three miles from town is the mesa. An immense and solitary wedge, the mesa squats on the plain like some German battleship that had been driven to the ends of the ocean where, out of fuel and cornered by His Majesty's cruisers, it was scuttled in shallow waters by its bedeviled Kapitän.

The town lay to the mesa's starboard beam, as it were. Supposing for a moment the existence of a bow rail at the mesa's foredeck, and supposing you leaned at that rail looking south, you'd see Santa Juana, down and away, adrift on the desert floor like a simmering, half-swamped raft. Between the mesa and the town ran the Santa Juana River, and along the river ran the highway, and from the mesa you could see many miles of either one as they trailed away in tandem toward the horizon. But nobody drives the highway these days, like I said. And the river dried up years ago, its cutbanks burrow-riddled and patrolled by coyotes.

When I was a kid, a few trailers were parked, haphazard-like, on the top of the mesa. "Haphazard": that's a good word. "Haphazard" being the default mode of much human endeavor in places like this, where there's so much space that a cow or a trailer strikes the passerby as either stranded or abandoned, even if it isn't.

People, too, give a like impression. Consider the man leaning on the guardrail beside the interstate today, some miles east of Gallup, resting his hands on his knees. He has a rolled gray blanket hanging from his shoulder like one of Lee's rebels on the eve of Appomattox. And like the rebel, he hasn't seen a square meal in days.

Or the man walking down the shoulder, who holds a sign at arm's length. The sign's message, facing the upcoming traffic, reads DEAD HORSE—which is not a prophecy, as we know, but a place. In Arizona.

Or the young couple standing in the scrub beside Route 9, some winter afternoon, shielding one another from the wind. Perhaps they're headed for one of those small towns with a Navajo name—Nakaibito or Iyanbito or Tohatchi—the kind of place where you can be certain that *somebody's* grandma lives, who is bound to let you in.

In every direction, as you look out from the mesa, are mountains, and beyond these is a sheer blank. To a nine-year-old boy, what lay on the other side of the mountains was irrelevant. The outside world amounted to little more than a scrap of frivolous gossip, for the mountains were the obstinate demarcation of all possible knowledge. It's in the nature of mountains to be terminal. They've made their minds up that there is, in fact, an end to things. If they spoke, it would be in Akkadian legalese, and we'd do well to follow their counsel.

In 1968, I went to live in my uncle's trailer, which was parked atop the aforesaid mesa. My uncle Edward was interesting in the way certain wild animals are interesting. He had what's called a "penetrating mind." That's not very illuminating, so I'll put it another way. Whatever caught his attention, he trained on it from every point of the compass. I mean to say that he thought *through* things. It would be a mistake to imagine this skill as salutary. From what I've seen of it, I wouldn't wish a penetrating mind on the lowest reprobate. It's the worst sort of affliction, a thing that won't be shut off. His mind churned, even when he sat in his aluminum chair with his eyes closed, an old miller minding his ghostly mill wheels.

What I'm describing, of course, is a fairly common strain of loneliness that lasted until he brought Molly home, and I'll talk about that presently. My uncle was a quiet man who never hurt a living creature or spoke ill of any person, but it was wearying to share a space with him. If I had known better, I'd have been a better companion, for whereas I had the whole mesa to wander, he was trapped in his own toils. But then, I was a kid, and no good company to nobody.

The thing that loomed largest in my uncle's eyes, the thing that blocked his sun—the thing that forbade the possibility of peace with the stonelike stubborn fact of itself—was a brokendown truck. The truck squatted thirty feet from the screen door in a patch of perpetually scuffed gravel, its hind wheels propped on blocks like a legless beggar on a skid. From its cracked and inconsolable headlamps, it gazed back at the man seated in the trailer's shadow and delivered its solemn indictment. My uncle suffered in the presence of that truck as one under a curse. They owned one another.

The desert is hard on restless souls like his, which is a paradox, since restless people—and restless peoples—seem to find their ways to the wilderness in numbers, and always have. He spent many days working on that truck, and when he wasn't turning a wrench in fact, he was turning one in theory, seated in his chair, two fingers drumming his chin. The toe of his boot tapped the sand with the weight of the moon as he peered from under the brim of his hat at that dumb beast of a machine. I swear the thing was inclined to drag itself away, if only to escape the torment of periodic interrogations with deep well sockets and ratchet extensions, pain that could match anything the Dominicans inflicted on the Free Spirit women.

One particular bolt had seized fast and mounted a bitter resistance. In the afternoon of the battle's second day, my uncle emerged from behind the trailer with a three-foot length of iron pipe, what mechanics call a breaker bar. He approached the truck like one of the imperial leg-breakers trudging up Calvary, determined to finish the job.

He climbed up on the engine, slipped the handle of a twelve-inch pipe wrench into the breaker, fitted the wrench teeth on the recalcitrant bolt and rocked with both feet on that bar, like a boy bounces on a branch that won't break. By lengthening the leverage, you see, he'd added torque to the applied pressure (it's one of the laws of physics, I think). Anyway, he stood on the engine, springing on the bar, damning Jesus Christ and His nearest kin to hell, as the poor truck wheezed on its spent springs.

How sorry I felt for them both at that moment. He freed up that bolt at last, and afterward stood sweating at the quarter panel, his feet planted once more on the earth. He reached out and gently tugged a plug cable and spoke quietly to the engine about how he'd hated to do it, but it was for its own good, and everything was gonna be easier now, you'll see.

I wandered off to find Fargo.

Fargo lived in a trailer on a corner of the mesa. His place, comprised of a horse corral and a compound of cannibalized vehicles, occupied one promontory like a thieves' camp. His place was mazy with wreckage, eminently defensible, with every approach well covered.

He owned a dozen horses that managed to keep alive out in the scrub, browsing the sharp sparse grass. Mornings or evenings, one or two horses might be seen standing on the edge of some forlorn arroyo, stirring the wind with their tails, manes falling over their ears and eyes, rapt to the wind.

On that particular day, I caught up with Fargo as he was calling his animals home. He spotted a lone creature on the skyline, a brief point of life browsing in silhouette, and we set off down the slope toward the horse.

On the way, as he often did, he shared a story, and it went like this. Horses had lived in this place for hundreds of years, a hundred generations of horses whose forebears had endured monthslong voyages in the damp and reeking holds of wooden ships that had sailed from Cádiz and Finisterre to Jamaica and Vera Cruz, where the sick and famished survivors were led ashore, there to be rewarded—if they didn't collapse and die on the beach—with caparisons of regal velvet and crimson plumes that nodded over their ears.

Those horses carried the conquistadors, Fargo explained, northward through Sonora and the Lion Mountains, past the silver towns of the central highlands, across the River of the North in search of the Seven Cities of Gold that had been founded by the seven renegade Portuguese bishops. Those horses grew inured to hardship, to smoke and cannonfire and the odor of spilt blood.

Fargo gestured toward the highway and said, Look along there, the Spaniards used to pass this way between Mexico City and the missions of Rio Arriba.

It was a true story, for the weather changed in the telling of it, and the wind, as he spoke, goaded a pack of dust hounds across our path, hounds let slip once more by their soldier-masters. As he spoke of the Spaniards' grim progress through the land, I envisioned a file of men decked in corroded silver armor, their faces fixed in weariness and thirst. I saw them leading starved horses that were draped with scarlet saddle blankets and panniers full of piñon nuts and turquoise, beneath a sun that is both the same and not the same as ours.

And when we finally stood beside Fargo's horse, I believed for a moment that I could read her thoughts, and she knew that I knew at least one of her secrets. My presence made her impatient, and she snorted in resentment at the disruption of her noon devotions. Her pedigree, steeped in fire and agony, lent her a nobility that would not be comforted, not by me.

◆

Fargo had the genial melancholy of a man who spent several hours a day thinking. He wore the flamboyant moustache of the disinherited hidalgo. It seemed he had plenty of time on his hands and was content to let it expire as it listed.

Certainly, he read many books, but he never, so far as I recall, mentioned any titles, nor did I ever actually see him reading. He was one, I suspect, for whom reading, like prayer, was a talking with ghosts, to be conducted in private.

The most ardent readers I've encountered commune in solitude with books in the same way others might commune with the darker powers, and a few readers, for this reason, bear a touch of shame about it. To read a book on history is to invoke the dead, to summon buried knowledge with no intention of sharing it. Mysterious habits indulged in isolation will always, no matter what they are, earn the covert hostility of our neighbors. The act of reading—reading history above all—will appear as a rejection of the dear hallucinations embraced by the general rout of respectable citizens, who prefer human experience to be tidily encapsulated in a few specious pronouncements such as *what's done is done* and *the past is past* and *water under the bridge* and other suchlike expressions of indiscriminate malarkey.

✦

Fargo had the gift—one my uncle didn't share—for fixing things. One day, as we sat in the flickering shade of the aspen tree that flourished in the midst of Fargo's decommissioned fleet, he told me about his long tuition in enginery.

Kid, I was *named* after a truck, he said to me. The day the government men took me off to that school, two things happened. They shaved my head, and they made me trade my name for a regular one. That was kind of tricky, he said, so I wrote home to my father, asking what my school name oughtta be, because the school people need to know right away. Now, my father had a truck, you see, a 1932 Plymouth Fargo, an old Forest Service wagon he bought at a government auction. Kept the thing humming for many years. That's how I learned to fix engines. Me and my father broke that thing down to the rivets a hundred times, and a hundred times we put it back together—me and him—each time better than before.

And with that he took a conclusive swallow from his beer bottle. Around us, the jacked and hoodless wrecks with their busted windscreens seemed to hearken, as best they might, to their master's voice.

But something had gotten lost in the telling of the tale, so I waited a polite interval, then reminded Fargo of the original topic.

Right you are, kid! I was talking about being named for a truck, wasn't I? My father, he sends a one-word note to me at the school: Fargo. That's all the note said. *Fargo*. So I showed it to the schoolmasters, and that became my school name. I still use it. It's just easier, some places, like here. You understand. Or maybe you don't.

By now, I could see that his mind was back in those past times. While he was there, he told me another story, one that has remained in my heart all these years.

I spent six years in that miserable place, he said. On the last day of school, the principal spoke some words. They read our names and they gave us our papers. The moment we could get away, all the boys and girls ran together into the pine woods, to a small clearing that was known only to us, out of earshot and out of sight of the teachers. We formed a circle and held hands, danced the round dance, sang the old songs. That day was the best day of my life. We were just so damn happy to be free.

I'll always be grateful to Fargo for sharing that story. I can picture the day so clearly in my mind, an afternoon as a poet might compose it: pines and sunlight, the *bee-loud glade* and the yellow flowers, the gin-scent of sap and the terrible, heartbreaking joy.

I never thought to ask Fargo what his birth name was, and that oversight remains one of my sorest regrets in this life. I would write a letter and ask him, even today. But he departed this ground long ago.

🔹

Many men spend their whole lives trying to fix stuff. Engines, toilets, radios, roofs; families, marriages. But the better part of these men, perhaps most, have no talent for it, and they know it. The grace and confidence of the dexterous ones inspire grief and envy in the hearts of the ungifted. To the latter's way of thinking, only one task has been allotted to the children of men by the Creator in his inscrutable wisdom, and that is *to manage machines*. To fail in this task is to fail in the one thing that gives meaning to life and legitimacy to manhood. For these unfortunates, the road to death will be littered with stripped bolts and empty cans of roof tar, and the grave will open to receive them with the cold breath of pipe dope and scorched plug cables.

That rare talent for tools, not to be acquired from repair manuals, endows a person with an easy slang for objective truths, and an imperishable air of calm and approachability. Someone who is good at fixing things will rarely be long without an income or a companion, and for this reason they're seldom found in a sour mood. Such a one, like Fargo, has leisure to burn, and he'll spend an hour without stint on any friendly soul who happens by, even a nine-year-old boy like me. Especially me, I'd say, because he could tell me things that would make more sophisticated ears ring.

Impoverished gentleman-journeymen like him, who wander the earth with a pair of wire-strippers and a flashlight in their back pockets, remind me of those over-leveraged squires who haunt the margins of Victorian novels, perpetually semi-inebriated and cheerfully unfazed by paternity claims. Fargo was better adapted to modern life than my uncle, though like my uncle, Fargo was a poor man too. Most people in Santa Juana were. I doubt Fargo had the money to have his own body buried. And being a philosophical soul, he'd probably consider it a good deed to die in debt, like those pious Roman Christian women did in the days when sticking it to the rich was theologically defensible and might even get you beatified.

Fargo belonged to that sort of whom society says, with a resentful admiration: *he just breezes through life*. It's a wonderful phrase, and it gladdens me to find someone on whom to bestow it, though these occasions are rare enough.

Therefore, times when my uncle raged at his poor dumb truck, I wandered over to Fargo's place. I'd stay till sundown when he set his beer aside to whistle for his horses. One evening, they came headlong out of the windy, wine-colored light, like they were rounding the bend at Saratoga Springs. As the ten of them closed the distance at full stride, Fargo took up his position at the entrance to his corral, puffing casually on a Winston.

The earth trembled at the horses' approach, and I vanished behind a gatepost.

Fargo set himself like a cornerback, crouched on planted feet, divining the proper angle with his lead shoulder. The horses broke over him like the sea and he disappeared in a cloud. When the dust cleared, there he stood, twenty feet from where he'd been a moment earlier, holding a bridle in his hand, whispering hard into one horse's ear, the cigarette still burning in his teeth. The other horses stood around, ears pivoting, snorting and snuffing, wondering why they weren't running anymore.

One day I found him standing out near the edge of the mesa, looking down the slope at a horse. I stepped up beside him.

A man who didn't know any better, he said without turning, would say that horse is pregnant.

The horse stood in the greasewood, far below, head bowed and quite still. I followed Fargo down the slope. When we arrived, he patted the horse's back and rump as he circled her, talking aches and weather to the animal, the way people do when they share their workaday troubles. He lifted the animal's tail and pushed his hand into the anus, slowly to the elbow, whispering the while. He pivoted his arm, now shoulder-deep in the horse's butt, and swept out a shovel-load of green shit, which was followed by three more shovel-loads that splattered Fargo's boots. When he swatted the horse's rump, by god, that beast fairly skipped away. Fargo, green to the bicep, stood watching with a look of doubtful serenity.

Horses get constipated, kid, he said. Just like people.

We returned to his trailer, where I poured water from a bucket over his arm. He shook it dry, put on a new shirt, and fetched a can of beer for himself and one for me.

We sat on aluminum chairs at the mesa's edge and kept a lazy watch on the highway. It was deserted, as usual, all the way to the mountains.

A desert highway will begin to vanish if you watch it long enough. Up close it seems a proper token of industrial enterprise, triumph of the machine age, seemingly ineradicable. One can observe how the earth has been leveled and graded, two layers of asphalt laid and tarred at the seams and hems, all of it nicely bedded, a changeless thing in a changeless desert. A thing of permanence it is, a stake in the future.

But follow with your eyes as the road ascends the bajada and wends through the benched hills into the mountains. It soon acquires the appearance of something makeshift and provisional. As perspective widens, it becomes clearer that the desert determines the highway, and not otherwise. The road resembles a strip of tape like surveyors might nail to the desert floor, a tape growing more attenuated with distance. Farther on, the ribbon of road shimmers, blinks twice, then it's gone.

Someone's walking along the highway, Fargo said. See?

It took a moment to locate the small object moving with grim resolution through the vastity of the basin. For an hour we marked the object's progress, which changed position when I wasn't looking, in the canny way a cloud does, or a star. As the thing homed along the highway, the land reared in silence at either hand to track its every step, and by and by the object grew until it assumed the inimitable locomotion of a far-ranging biped.

A woman or man, oblivious to the paradox of itself. To watch someone cross open land is to partake of the illusion that one human being, by dint of their relative littleness, is trivial and inconsequential. It is only with time and experience that one arrives at the truth that a single one of these tiny creatures, of its own volition, possesses powers sufficient to overshadow many deserts.

The figure turned off the highway at the foot of the mesa and began its slow ascent through the scrub, resolving into the figure of a woman crossing the level ground toward the very place where we sat.

At last, like a harassed and shabby courier, she came to a halt in front of Fargo and delivered the message that she had traveled so far, and at such cost, to convey.

Fargo, she said. My fuckin car's broke down.

What is it?

Flat.

Did you gash the sidewall or puncture the tread?

Fucked if I know. Can you help me out, man?

Fargo stood and offered his chair. You need a beer first.

That's a fact. Who's the kid?

He's my assistant.

I'm Raymond, I said.

They thought that was funny. I don't know why.

⚬

I sat in the cab between them holding a black satchel resembling a country doctor's bag that contained, not hemostats and smelling salts, but tools. Fargo had a device he'd made from a vacuum cleaner motor, which he could plug into the cigarette lighter of a car. Say you had a flat and no spare. He'd come to your car and plug the puncture with a pair of forceps and a wad of rubber and refill the tire with that home-made air compressor. And if the rim was bent, he'd beat on it with a framing hammer, listen for air, and beat some more until it sealed. No need for a wrecker. He just tossed his satchel into the cab of his truck and fixed your trouble, same day, roadside. He owned a stockade of junked cars, and he could generally switch out a thermostat or a fuel pump, if it came to that. And on those rare occasions when he couldn't mend the vehicle on the spot, he'd drag the thing on a chain up the mesa to his stockade, where its destiny was either to be revived for a fee, or dissected for usable parts.

We drove out to the woman's car and Fargo plugged the tire, all the while making jokes about Oldsmobiles that were lost on me and her. She gave him five bucks and a promise to bring over a few beers next

Saturday, to make up the difference. He had a sense for stranded travelers. I don't know how the word got to them, but Fargo's name somehow reached the ears of nearly every stranger who managed to break down within Santa Juana County limits. Neither do I know if this woman ever did return with those beers she owed him. I only remember this moment at all, I suppose, because it happened only days before Molly arrived.

When I returned to my uncle's place that evening, I found him wiping the black palm prints off the quarter panels where he'd leaned all day peering into the engine. He'd been waiting. He smiled when he saw me and immediately got behind the wheel.

Stand right there, nephew, he said.

He turned the key. His eyes lit when the engine turned over. He sat in the cab, buried in the roar, toeing the gas, grinning at the miracle of noise in a place that had known only the wind since winter. He was buttoned at wrist and neck in a red shirt, and I noticed he'd combed his moustache and brushed it smooth with sugar-water, the way some men used to do. I stood beside the driver's door as he shouted, fierce and proud.

Do you think the world stopped spinning, he called down to me, while I was neck-deep in this thing? Do you think everything stopped while I battled, nephew? Why should the world stop spinning while my back is turned?

I didn't know what he was talking about. He wrenched the gear shift into reverse.

I'll be back in two days, he said. There's enough food in there. You go to Fargo if any trouble happens, all right? I gotta go get Molly.

He fishtailed down the track toward the highway, tires kicking stones. I went inside and stalked flies with a rolled-up copy of the *Santa Juana Chronicle*, wondering who Molly was.

I didn't know where Molly came from. Nor did I know, at that time, why my uncle brought her to the trailer on the mesa outside Santa Juana. Maybe he assumed that a trailer ought to have a woman in it, who could keep things in order and at peace. He may have had a notion that a boy ought to have a female around, in order to alleviate its upbringing.

It's funny. Most of us are visited, sooner or later, by some mysterious compulsion to explain ourselves to somebody. In most lives there comes a point when you just got to come clean. And the one you come clean to, well, now they own a piece of you, and you own a piece of them. Marriage has its roots in this—what do I call it?—biological necessity.

It may be that Molly answered that need of my uncle's, and he of hers.

But in this case, I believe, Molly and my uncle made a mutual discovery that, marriage or no marriage, they needn't explain anything at all about themselves. The past, whatever it contained, went without saying, and the need to come clean was rendered redundant.

Such a recognition is nothing more than evidence of the mysterious hidden ground of pain that bears up every love—ground that calls out to ground, just as the deep, in the ancient song, calls unto deep. What a fortunate thing it is, when past sins and bad choices become dispensable; when acceptance, in that felicitous phrase, *goes without saying.*

Forgiveness springs from the need to be forgiven and acceptance from the desire to be accepted. Let it be observed that the sinless among us have few close friends and fewer untroubled marriages. In the last analysis, we're all guilty as hell. It's best to embrace that.

I mention these things because, for the brief time they spent together, so far as I could tell, Molly and my uncle Edward made a peaceful union of mutual kindness and respect—one marked by an aptitude for sitting quietly together, side by side.

When she stepped out of the truck that day, Molly stepped into a place my uncle had spent many years preparing, the way a very discriminating bird might fashion a nest, knowing little of the individual that would come to dwell in it, but secure in the knowledge that, when they did arrive, they would share his language and his worries, a cup of coffee and the evening's first star.

Neither of them would have put the thing into these words. Had anyone told them such lunacy as I'm talking now, Molly would have been alarmed, and my uncle annoyed.

Two days after my uncle left, he returned as promised. I was sitting in the trailer when I heard the high-pitch, low-gear grind of the old truck. The engine gunned up the track, firing on every cylinder like a beast shouting its name. Though the windshield dust obscured the cab's occupants, I could discern two shadows behind the glass. The truck stopped and they got out.

In the cool morning sunshine, Molly stood holding a brown satchel in her hand by way of luggage. She wore a faded field jacket and dusty sandals and her red hair tied at the nape. My uncle saw my face at the window and waved at me, and I came out and shook Molly's hand. She said hi and I said hi, and in her smile was an assurance that she was not the sort to rat people out, so there was no need to worry. I could tell by her clothes that she didn't have any hang-ups about befriending a small boy.

My uncle showed Molly around the trailer. She stowed her bit of gear. They shared a coffee and a quiet chat, and our home, just like that, was hers.

That day, while my uncle worked on the truck, Molly asked me to take her around, so we set off into the desert. We analyzed bird tracks, investigated a hollowed barrel cactus and its resident long-winged flies, talked about bobcats, the way people do.

In the evening of Molly's first day, she and my uncle sat on aluminum chairs placed side by side in the sand, and she held his hand in

her lap. Neither spoke as the red tide of sundown ebbed over the skyline, leaving a jetsam of stars like broken shells on a beach.

This became the ritual. From that day on, they sat together and
watched the great gothic drama that plays for free most evenings in
the desert sky. I often sat with them, and they accepted my presence
with unspoken contentment. And if I was late for the show, Molly
called to me to join them.

Those sunsets, in time, seem to ripen to an unearthly vividness,
and with the years they grow more lovely in my mind.

⁂

That silver trailer we lived in, we called *the sleeper*. Fargo gave it that
name because it was long and silver and resembled a sleeper car such
as you could still find, in those waning days of rail travel, trundling
along the Atchison line.

The month that Molly arrived, the country was in the grips of
spring. Freezing winds arrived night or day to beat on the sleeper like
a person might take a knotted towel to an upturned canoe.

One night, the wind blew so hard the sleeper rocked like a duck
boat on an autumn lake, and I feared the thing would tip. The panels
fanned and burred, the jars rattled, the windows whistled. I lay on the
floor by the stove as silver phantoms of wind-light swept across the ceiling.

Through the window fell a slender beam of moonlight—planed
smooth and iron-blue. The beam stood canted on the floor like a
caved rafter. As the sleeper and all its contents shuddered, the beam
alone did not tremble, but fixed the sleeper to the earth like a silver eel
pierced by a celestial fish spear. For this reason, and to this day, it's
gratitude I feel whenever I see the moon.

I can still see the three of us clearly, in my heart's eye, asleep or
awake in that windshaken thing, the crew of an unmoored and ill-
christened craft.

Those nights, Molly made my uncle keep the stove on. He resisted because he was careful about things that cost money, but he relented because he was cold. He had to make a brief show, for our benefit, of being tougher than the temperature, as men sometimes do, until such pretenses become tiresome even to themselves.

The stove was the size of a breadbox and came from the Army surplus store in Albuquerque. A fuel line ran from the stove through the trailer's siding to an upturned jerrycan of diesel just outside. My uncle rigged a scaffold so that the can, from its elevated position, served as a gravity tank. The line was fitted with a valve that allowed a single drop, every other second or so, to drip into the burning stove, which kept the fire alive. The stove grumbled all night like a caged animal being tormented with a pointy stick—a low mean sound. Sometimes I wished we didn't keep the stove on during windy nights, because everyone knew how Virgil Suarez got blown up. The wind shook his trailer so hard it snapped the line between his stove and the fuel tank outside, and the gas puddled on the floor while he was sleeping.

My uncle once showed me photographs of the atom bomb tests that happened in the desert to the south. I imagined Virgil's trailer going up in a similar cloud. As a kid, I believed that everything that blew up blew up that way. Now I know different. But then, as I lay on the mattress on the floor on a given windy night, watching that charmed fuel line shiver, miniature fiery mushroom clouds rose like hot-air balloons in my mind.

Every spring in that part of the world, the wind blows. When it isn't blowing, it idles out on the desert, biding its time, making likenesses in its own image and setting them loose—one here one there—spinning devils like a drunk spins a coin. In the daytime, I tried to run inside the devils so I could learn what it meant to be caught up in a whirlwind, but the things always stepped aside, and I could never reach one in time. If I came close, it evaded me—or it vanished, suddenly sapped of spin as though somebody had pulled its plug. And when the devil died, the component sand settled scattercast over the ground, leaving no trace of itself. Nearby, however, another devil was sure to be spinning, and I'd set off at a run. But it too dissolved or whirled away.

The dust turned the day orange and you might see the doubled slash of headlights from a truck beating down the highway, or someone walking headlong on the shoulder, and the whole day and the whole world seemed to drain into the bleary puddle of the sun for hours.

I loved the wind, but I never told anyone. There were many who didn't share my affection.

◆

Molly had been at the trailer for about a month when the wildfires broke out. In the distance, by day, the smoke smeared the skyline. If the wind was right, the sky turned hazy gray and the sun turned a cool yellow, so dull you could look right at it without crying.

The wildfire sunsets became outrageous affairs, splendors of penny and brick-dust. Evenings, we could see the long unartful sutures of the fire lines across the mountain's face. At night these lines scored the middle air, like arrested strokes of lightning, flaring and glistering along their lengths. I had to look away, then peer back, to register the fact that the fires were creeping slowly up the slopes, relentless as the tide.

The fires made my uncle uneasy. He grew more-than-usually quiet. I crouched beside him one afternoon as he sat cross-legged in the sand and contemplated the lotus of an exposed brake rotor. When I asked him where Molly had come from, the question seemed to call him back from another world.

She's from El Paso, he said. She worked in a diner there. I asked her to come live with us and she said yes. You see, nephew, he said, as he ran his thumb across the ugly grooves that had scored the rotor's plate—You see, nephew, she was in hell and I took her away. Now this place aint no Eden, but it is an improvement on Texas.

Maybe not a big improvement, he added with a glance at the ashen sky.

I was proud of my uncle for saving Molly from an awful fate. I imagined him carrying her on his shoulders, like Aeneas carried his old father out of burning Troy. I pictured her, dressed in a soiled apron and checkered blouse, with two Ticonderoga pencils stuck like chopsticks in the red bun of her hair like a disreputable geisha.

El Paso must be a frightening place, I thought.

Uncle, I asked, am I gonna go to a school?

School? He frowned at the word. There aint no school no more, nephew. The schools've been disbanded.

He gave me a hopeless look and said, Molly reads to you. That's better than school. I'll ask her to teach you the sums. She's from the cities, you know. I bet she's seen a hundred schools.

⬤

The mountains had burned for five days; the fires were spreading. The yellow plume towered; the horizon vanished. The creeping lines of the fires were punctuated with flashes whenever a pine exploded.

In darkness, the fires glittered. Not in brief lines, as at first, but a growing skein of fires now, a hatchwork gradually knitting the slopes together. Blazes flared here and there like a pot on a low boil. And the rains were not due for months.

One morning, a pickup thundered up the lane to the trailer. Three men sat in the bed, weathered rucksacks piled at their feet. Axe and shovel handles lay athwart the gate like a brace of muskets. The handles were banded high and low with black electrical tape, and in between these bands the wood was stained to ebony where it had been gripped tight in sweaty fists for days.

The men sat in dour silence with faraway expressions. My uncle exchanged a word with the driver, then came inside, stuffed some items of clothing and food in a pack, slung a rolled woolen blanket over his shoulder, and paused in front of Molly. He placed his hand on her elbow and spoke briefly, with a glance at me. She nodded. He kissed her cheek, left the trailer door open on his way out, climbed into the truck bed, and claimed his place among the others.

That day, Molly and me sat together at the table and consulted the trailer's library, a lone picture book called *Indian Tribes of North America.* We lingered over an illustration of a hunter draped in wolfskin, clutching bows in either hand, creeping up the blind side of a slow rise. Beyond the rise is a vast sea of bison spilling over the horizon. But the hunter could not see the animals yet—only we could see them. The picture had a way of granting privilege to secret information that was important to no one but Molly, the bowhunter, and myself. The secret bewitched me.

I bet he gets one, Molly said, tapping a bison that grazed beyond the hunter's view. I heard, she said, that a buffalo gave you everything you needed to live on. Food, clothes. Lots of other things.

What other things, Molly?

Everything, she said. What I wouldn't do with a buffalo, Ray Moon!

From first to last, Molly called me Ray Moon. I didn't know whether it was a matter of mishearing, or some quirk of city speech, or just a fancy of hers, but she never called me anything else, and I never thought to correct her. To her I was Ray Moon, that's all.

What I wouldn't do with a buffalo, Ray Moon! We'd make two blankets out of him, she said, and have meat all winter. I heard their tongue is valuable. We could trade a tongue in town for money and chocolate and maybe some brandy. Ah, I wish I had some brandy. Just a nice small glass is all.

She looked out the window toward the mountains, and the fires looked back.

Molly heated a can of beans on the stove, and I made a peanut butter sandwich and cut it in two. We sat at the open book, overlooking a picture, and did not turn the page for fear of soiling the book with breadcrumbs.

That night we sat outside with my uncle's empty chair between us.

▬

No one came to the trailer the next day or the one after that. On the third day, a pickup climbed slowly up the lane, but it was no messenger from the fires. A man in a cowboy hat climbed out of the pickup as we walked out to greet him. Instead of the yellow evergreen of the Forest Service, the word BOOKS was stenciled in black on both doors and on the tailgate.

I'm the book lender, he said to Molly. I come up this way every few months if I can keep the truck on the road. You're welcome to swap a book for a book, if you got any to hand, or you can buy one outright. The money I take, he said, goes pry-merrily into the gas tank. If you don't have a book to swap nor money to buy one, I will take an IOU and we can settle up some other day. If you're a book type person, you might want to stock up while you can, cause my jurisdiction covers Navajo Land clear away to Pecos and the towns and counties in between. That's all by way of saying that weeks might pass before you see this truck again.

The three of us gathered at the tailgate. Many of the books piled in the bed of the truck bore county library stamps: Cibola County and San Juan County and Oñate County. The word DISCARDED was stamped in red on the title page of the first book I opened. Some came from faraway libraries, I noticed, as I leaned over the panel and fished about. The heap smelled as if it'd gotten rained on during Eisenhower's time and spent the last ten years drying out. Denver Public Library, Gallup High School Library, Municipal Library of Roswell, Durango Municipal Library, Public Library of Amarillo. There was one from West Albuquerque Elementary, and one from The Public Libraries of Tucson.

The book truck itself was a high country circuit rider, all crumpled corners and bald tires. Sprays of dried mud flared from the wheel wells like the gold wings on Mercury's boots.

As we picked at covers, the man stood between us and praised this and that.

This one will teach you French, he said, then tossed the book back when it failed to further recommend itself.

Now look at this here, daughter, he said, *Good Manners for Modern Children.*

He handed the book to Molly.

She subjected the thing to a hopeful inspection, searching for an excuse to like it, then handed it back. I'm afraid we're not modern children, she said.

Look, Ray Moon! Molly said. Here's a book I bet you like.

It was called *The Zuni Indians*, written by a man named Stevenson, and it bore the stamp of the Window Rock School Library. It was singed and stiff, as though it had been subjected to the ordeal for harboring heterodoxical beliefs.

There was a time—many centuries ago, back when eunuchs serenaded the popes—when a book condemned for heresy would be publicly burnt by imperial executioners in the marketplaces. Picture a beefy hangman in a black hood holding an armload of books like it's his first day of school.

Molly and the book man smiled, patiently waiting for me to do something with this man Stevenson and his book.

It looks interesting, Molly said. Read us some lines, Ray Moon. Go on.

I leafed to a random page and read aloud: *The sun rose in splendor on the morning of the fifth day, making brilliant the mantle of snow that covered the earth. The valley was sparkling white, and the mesa walls were white, with here and there a patch of dark blue, the pines veiled by the atmosphere. The snowy plain—*

How beautiful! Molly said.

The boy reads good, said the book man, not a little surprised.

He asked me if I liked butterflies and I said yes, so he gave me a book, *Biotic Survey of the Great Basin*, which had been discarded from some place called St. George College. I didn't know where St. George College was, but I knew that book had traveled a long distance in its time. That book isn't finished traveling, either, for I've carried it with me to this day.

Molly and me had finished the *Indian Tribes* book by now, so I ran inside and fetched it and gave it to the book man.

That'll be *Biotic Survey* and *Zuni Indians,* he said. One free swap and one purchase.

He jotted figures on the wheel well with a stub pencil. It was then I noticed that the truck's rear quarter panel was crawling with rain-faded mathematical calculations: hieroglyphics in miniscule, and all in pencil.

The book man said, That's forty-five cents, son. You want to pay now or later?

Molly dug a few coins from her field jacket pockets and handed them over, and she and the book man shared a laugh about money that didn't include me. But I didn't stay miffed for long, for we had founded a legitimate library of two books. And *both* volumes were illustrated.

The man handed Molly a business card, by way of a slip of paper, bearing the words REGINALD WILLIE, BOOK LENDER, NAVAJOLAND & ENVIRONS, printed in pencil in a meticulous script.

As the truck rattled off down the lane, we stood side by side in the sunlight and leafed through the nature book, where we found sketches of spiders and wildflowers, cactus and lichen, junipers and bats and lizards. There wasn't a living thing on earth but found its image, I believed, in the *Biotic Survey*, and Molly read my thoughts.

This book has the whole universe in it, Ray Moon! she said.

⏤

That same afternoon, an apple-green truck, bearing the familiar stenciled yellow evergreens on its doors, rolled to a stop in front of the trailer. Two unshaven men got out of the cab. One man wore outsize yellow canvas trousers hitched with blue suspenders, like the fireman from the Smokey Bear billboards. His sleeves were rolled, revealing forearms blackened to the wrist, though his big hairy hands were clean. The second man's sleeves were buttoned neat, and his hands, I noticed, were also clean.

You're Molly, said the second man.

Yes. Have you been to the fires? Have you been to the mountains? Have you been with Edward?

The man looked at me. Is this Edward's nephew?

That's Ray Moon.

Is he your son?

He's mine, Molly said.

The men shared a glance. Molly, the second man said, Will you take a walk with me?

She started forward with him, cautiously, as though a false move might shatter something, and they wandered together with heads bowed, until she stopped in her tracks. The big-handed fireman guided me by the shoulder toward the chairs, where we took seats. What's your name? Ray Moon?

No, it's what Molly calls me. My name's Raymond.

Why's she call you that then?

I don't know. She might think it's my name.

I see. Which one do you like?

Both are okay, I guess.

The man spit politely to the side, laced his fingers, looked toward the faraway smoke. He scowled and spit once more, something bitter in his throat. The blue skies shaded to sulfur where they vaulted the simmering mountains.

I'm afraid it's bad news, Ray, the man said.

⚊

That day and the next, Molly sat beside the window and watched the mountains that smoldered like a wicked city. On the third morning, the firemen returned in the Forest Service truck and waited as we washed our faces and combed our hair.

They made space for us in the cab, and we drove to the cemetery, a fenceless tract of hard ground a mile from town, where we found a dozen uneven rows of bird-stained stones, and sun-varnished wooden crosses guarded by the chipped plaster figurines of saints.

One cross, away in a corner, was surrounded by smoke-rimmed, rose-tinted candle jars that glinted, not with candleflames, but with desert light. Adorned with a green sprig of juniper, this cross—alone among the many faded and unattended ones—seemed to flourish in its little wild garden of sun-shot glass.

The cemetery was situated in a tract of low ground. Shut away from all prospect of the surrounding land, our vision was restricted on every side to the bare slopes of a depression whose rim gathered the sky into a deep violet pool, the depths of which remained untroubled by smoke and ash.

Beside the firefighters and Molly, only a few people from town were present as the priest smiled and signed a cross over the missal in his hand. He stood on one side of the turned grave, and we on the other, and he spoke in a dead tongue that I didn't understand. But I knew that the words had been spoken uncountable times, and that therein lay a good deal of their authority.

Requiem aeternam dona eis, Domine, et lux perpetua luceat eis

I did not know how it could be that these windburnt men and women, who probably owned no more than two sets of clothes apiece— one for work and one for days like this—had contrived to master discrete languages for discrete occasions. It seemed a power verging on sorcery. Only later did I realize that most of them understood little more than I did.

Te decet hymnus Deus, in Sion, et tibi reddetur votum in Jerusalem: exaudi orationem meam, ad te omnis caro veniet

The words were neither comforting nor sad. There was, rather, a somber certainty to them. They seemed at home in this stony ground, and doubtless had their roots in such a place.

The words had lost their currency long ago, but not, somehow, their savor, for they had dwelt in this land for centuries—the legacy of barefoot friars whose numbers dwindled with the generations—to eke out a meager but dependable trade in the local mortality.

Nolumus vos ignorare de dormientibus, ut non contristemini, sicut et ceteri, qui spem non habit

Death's jargon was a costly hoard, a brittle paraphernalia to be removed from its gilt box on rare occasions and displayed to the aging faithful. There was a time when the chantry priest could demand exorbitant fees for such troubles. But the salad days of requiem Latin have passed.

A stray wind tugged, with a momentary gentle insistence, at the priest's black vestments as he spoke. *Absolve, Domine, animas omnium fidelium defunctorum ab omni vinculo delictorum*

The first man and woman, according to an old story, named the things around them—leaf, bird, fox—and each newly-named thing cast a shadow on the as-yet-unnamed things around it. And as each thing received its name, one by one by one, a living darkness crept over the land, until the whole world simmered in the half-light of a precarious knowledge.

The first woman and the first man discovered that the act of naming had a way of revealing the souls of things, but—by some sleight of the mind or of God—as the named things multiplied, so did the loneliness of those who named them. They kept naming things, however, because time does legitimize even the meanest habits.

Resurget frater tuus

In this way did their solitude increase, until loneliness became their chief possession, a dear and reliable companion, the only thing they understood absolutely.

A language, I've learned, is like a makeshift shelter, one generally adequate for protection from the elements. But it leaks sometimes, and it cannot stand in a storm. A time will come when the shelter I've so carefully constructed will afford me no security anymore, and at that point God will place his hand upon my mouth, and there will be an end to speech.

Praesta, quaesumus omnipotens Deus: ut anima famuli tui Edward, quae
hodie de hoc saeculo migravit, his sacrificiis purgata, et a peccatis expedita,
indulgentiam pariter et requiem capiat sempiternam

The firefighters commenced to fill the grave with the same black-banded shovels they had carried to the fires. The cutting edges of the shovelheads gleamed: self-sharpened from slicing gravel and hot sand, limned with silver from biting stone. One of the men handed Molly an envelope. Without opening it, she handed it to me. Inside was close to a hundred dollars in fives and ones and tens, wrinkled but neat like a waterlogged deck of cards.

The priest climbed into the truck with the diggers. The truck idled as the driver waited to take us home, but Molly begged the men off, and they departed without a word. We stood beside the grave as the roar of the truck faded to echoes resounding from unseen cliffs.

Did you bring something? Molly asked.

We sat cross-legged beside the mound of turned earth. I unfolded the map I'd made and pressed it to the sand. It represented a collation of geographical facts that I had garnered from the *Indian Tribes* book while it was in our possession. The nations' lands were designated, their names underscored: Kiowa, Snake, Hopi, Ogalalla, Zuni, Tewa, Arapahoe. *Comanche* I underscored twice, for they were known to be intolerant of intruders. On the map, the Seminole were returned to the Everglades, and the Shawnee were back home along the Ohio. Bison hoof prints dotted the central prairies to memorialize the grasslands. On the map, too, were the long westering lines of the emigrant trails—the Bozeman, the Oregon, the Santa Fe—meandering with a weird logic through plains, deserts, mountains, inevitably toward the western seaboard. I smoothed the map onto the sand and weighted it at the cardinal points with stones.

I made that map for my uncle because it would behoove him to know where the bison and the trails were situated. At that age, you see, I had a dim notion that to die meant to go back in time. The years have not entirely disabused me of that suspicion.

Molly dug in her pockets and retrieved two box-end wrenches and placed them, along with a pair of mittens, onto the map, then rolled the map in a scroll and tied it with a brief length of baling twine. Lastly, she scratched a shallow divot at the foot of the wooden cross and laid the scroll precisely there, as in a bed. She covered it with sand and gravel and patted the little heap into place.

Over time I came to understand that Molly arrived at important decisions, such as this one, through an interchange of unaccountable considerations, just as meteorological factors like pressure, temperature, and moisture contrive the day's weather. That's not to say her actions would appear unreasonable to the person on the street. What I mean to say is, Molly's thoughts ran by peculiar paths, as though she'd never in her life been asked to explain herself, nor ever expected to be. The cast of her mind was fashioned to allow the big obvious fish to go free, and to snag the colorful little overlooked ones.

I don't know where he's going, Molly said. Wrenches'll come in handier than weapons, though. And a man can always use mittens out there. It'll get cold at night, I don't doubt.

When we returned to the sleeper we found a three-pound bag of rice and a sack of potatoes, a loaf of bread, two sacks of tortillas, a pouch of dried chilis and a can of coffee, stacked in a neat heap just inside the door.

Molly wrote a note of thanks and sent me off with it. I did not deliver it to him but left it tucked under a wiper blade. Few things were so hateful to Fargo as gratitude.

Rain visited the mountaintops and doused the fires with such simple economy as to make my uncle's death seem pointless. But it was no good to follow that particular thread, which unraveled without issue.

I returned to the cemetery, some days later, and found that someone had visited the grave. The sand had been swept aside, the wrenches and the mittens and the map were missing, and there was an indecisive mess of boot prints around the wooden cross. I sat and waited, but not even a breeze disturbed the surrounding hills or the sky.

I was not afraid of seeing my uncle's ghost; I was afraid it might speak to me. But then, I reasoned, a ghost would surely be ashamed to speak with a boy in the broad light of day. For that matter, it's always shameful for a ghost to speak in the light, just as it's shameful for an old man to speak in the dark.

I'd brought along a pair of socks and a nutcracker and a note informing him I hadn't forgotten about him. I laid these things in the same place and covered them just as Molly had.

It may be a bad idea to speak face to face with the dead, I thought, but it's okay to write a note to them, or sit in their company for a while, so long as you don't yammer or fidget.

My uncle was a good man. He took me in at my mother's request, when she needed a hospital bed, and he never said a word about it. Her infirmities, whether of mind or body, were kept hidden from me. Troubles were common enough in that place, then as now. There but for the grace of God: that's what people said, and by such shibboleths they sought to keep the wolves of soul-sickness from their doors.

Though it is not central to this story, I cannot allow my uncle's part to pass without a few more words. He was born in Oklahoma, at a place called Mingo Hill, same as my mother and all their siblings. The name Edward Collins will be found, I expect, on a registry of births in a file box in the basement of the Department of Vital Statistics in Oklahoma City, Oklahoma. If you checked for Collinses born between 1920 and 1930, you'd surely find a couple dozen that were christened Edward. He'd be one of those. He died in Santa Juana County, New Mexico, in 1968, and from Oklahoma to New Mexico is as far as he traveled in this life.

He probably made mistakes and may have died with regrets for the things he failed to achieve. His name will never grace a legion hall or a bus station, nor will it be chiseled onto a plinth at the park, among the names of benefactors or fallen heroes. He left no legacy to speak of and no money, only a few acts of kindness that will survive in the memories of a woman and a boy for as long as they live. Only then will his name perish. And if this eulogy rings a touch grimly, that is not my intention, for it is not by the deeds of the great and powerful, but by the awkward and unrequited decency of unheralded souls that humankind is borne along, for good or ill, to the unsayable end that awaits it.

Over the following days, while Molly took long walks in the desert, I paged through our picture books and waited for her to return, never entirely convinced that she would. But she did come back, each day about sundown, and we'd share a meal and listen together as the night offered up the few poor tunes from its repertoire: coyote cries, the whistle of the freight as it trundled across the desert, and the wind. Few in kind but infinitely various, these same few melodies, in artless harmony, played each night for nothing under the stars.

The night will give up its secrets, trivial as they might seem in the daylight, but one must sit still and listen for them, and that for a long while. Molly composed each night's vigil without a word, by a demonstration of patience that was, I believe, not instinctive but necessary to the life she knew. Her quietness was itself a kindly invitation—one I'd have been remiss to decline—to an observance broken only at intervals, when she raised a cup of cold coffee to her lips.

As we sat at the card table that stood beside the window, she'd close the book I was looking at and turn the light out. Then the seam between ourselves and the night did vanish, and the darkness would enter and cover us, quiet as the snow. We welcomed the dark, and the dark made itself at home.

Whether Molly thought at these times about god, or destiny, or the past, I couldn't say. Years later, I read in a book how, at the portal to each new day, there stand two barrels—a barrel of good fortune and a barrel of ill fortune—and Zeus attends them both with his dipper. Upon waking, you take your place in line, along with the rest of humanity, and before you can proceed into the light, Zeus pours a dram from each barrel into your government-issue tin cup. The proportions vary, according to his inscrutable whim, but every morning you are given a sample from both barrels, and drain it on the spot you must, else you may not pass into the waking day.

I bet Molly would laugh at that story. Then again, in her own way, she probably knew it as well as anyone.

Molly woke early in the morning, two weeks after the burial, and stood at the window brushing her hair, which she had neglected to do for days. Her face was serene as she dipped her head to the brush. She looked at me in the reflection as if I were a bit of welcome news. For me, that was enough to gild the day.

She knew I'd been to the grave, she knew what I'd seen there, and she was glad for it.

Let's do school today, Ray Moon. Bring out the biota book, she said—pronouncing it *the boyda book.*

I still have it, the Boyda Book, and that's how I call it, if only to myself. The phrase has a ritual ring to it, something pagan, or Bohemian (from the days when that word signified heresy not hedonism). *The Boyda Book.* The words may have served as the title to a collection of Druid psalms, and in truth it was filled with wonders. There's still sand grit buried deep between the pages, the grains of which retain a glimmer of sunlight from our bright and windy walks.

II

MOLLY DROVE THE TRUCK TO THE POST OFFICE. THE POSTAL worker emerged from the back room with a box that emitted a sound like a hundred rusty wheels and handed the box to an elderly man. When the man turned and saw our faces, he opened the lid for us. Inside were two dozen yellow chicks clamoring in the sudden light. Molly picked up one chick and held it out so I could run my finger over its downy head. It pipped and wriggled in profound agitation.

The man closed the lid. When Molly sought to return the chick, he shook his head and said, no, you keep it, child, it's yours.

She handed the chick to me for safekeeping. I strained to form with my fingers a cage whose bars would not bruise the little creature's bones, which I imagined to be hollow, as brittle as straw, and butter-yellow like its fluff.

As I carried the chick through the door, suddenly responsible for another creature's life and well-being, I felt the universe settle a touch more comfortably into its rightful arrangement. From what I've heard people say about having a child, I imagine it's like a rinsing of all the blurry windows of the mind, a cleansing that leaves you blinking at a world now luminous and new, a world that will never be the same, though neither a whit nor a mote has been moved out of its place. Holding a chick is not the same as holding one's own child, I know, but the distressful joy was, I have to believe, of a similar species.

I held the chick like one unused to his own hands. Lord, I'm sorry to say it, but I'd have let your good earth burn if it meant preserving one hair of Squeaky's fluff.

Well, of course I named it Squeaky. Molly approved. That was easy. Squeaky had been Squeaky from the foundation of the world. A helpless creature was presented to me, and my center of gravity shifted toward it, for that is in the nature of love. Love is a kind of sorcery, like a snake charmer's tune, whose fascination lies in its power to lift us clear out of ourselves. Surely the old man at the post office knew this, and he didn't need some jangly definition like I just gave. He would have been embarrassed by my weird talk of love and charmer's pipes. It's silly, sure, but I'll keep it.

There was a letter from her brother, which made Molly very glad, and she tucked it unopened into her pocket. As we crossed the lot toward the truck, a man called to her. I didn't turn to look but sat in the cab with the chick in my lap, trying to ease Squeaky's restiveness and growing impatient to get home.

I saw them in the passenger door mirror. The man stood near her and talked with his face close to hers, and he reached out and touched her hair. As the hair slipped through his fingers, she shook her head, as one might shake away a moth.

The sheriff's back was turned to the truck, so I couldn't see his face, but I did see the pistol belt, the silver piping down his charcoal-colored trouser seams. I saw how he leaned in like he was telling a dirty joke or encouraging a wavering accomplice. He convinced her of things, she assented, and he took out his wallet and handed her some bills.

She put a dollar of gas in the tank, but the engine didn't turn, so we left it at the pump and set off down the shoulder. As we walked, Squeaky found a quietus, or a deep exhaustion, in the fold of my coat. About a mile from town, a man driving a wrecker pulled over to offer a ride, and we climbed into the cab. Neither Molly nor the driver spoke as the radio played a song about some common trouble. It occurred to me, as I sat between the silent people, that I didn't know what part of the world Squeaky hailed from. Somewhere far away, I supposed. Maybe another world. Maybe Texas.

The voice on the radio sang a song about broken hearts and empty houses.

As we thundered down the road, Molly added her voice to the driver's humming, and both of their voices joined the nameless singer's, who had a voice like Oklahoma, all cornflower sky and wind-rocked powerlines. Molly liked to sing, and she sang in a burry timbre—a sleepy glad sound—as though she'd been taught to sing by the sort of transistor radios that play in car repair bays and diner kitchens.

The trio warmed to one another—the singer and the wrecker driver and Molly—and their song soon rivaled the roar of the tires and the wind.

Molly and the wrecker man knew all the words, and I assumed that everyone on earth knew all the words to that song, which must have been the catechism of some dead religion that only people of a certain age had undergone.

I felt sorry to be excluded from the knowledge of ages, as it was manifested in those lyrics, for such knowledge led not to wisdom or wealth, but was the very blood and bone of life. Only people who had walked on lonely roads at night could sing that song.

There are songs we know *by heart.* It's a lovely idiom.

That night the sheriff came to the sleeper. When the candy-apple red headlights lit up the window, Molly shooed me into the back room. He didn't bother to knock, but walked in talking in the voice of a man who didn't care what his shoes tracked in. He came prepared to take what he wanted and get angry in the taking. He didn't disappoint himself.

There is a strain of viciousness that is casual, lighthearted even, commonly booze-fueled, possessed of an appalling agility. That was his.

I did not hear footsteps so much as a creak-and-buckle that betrayed his presence. From behind the door, I imagined a specter in a black habit, wearing a monk's hood and a Sam Browne belt, gliding over the floor, withering everything with its gaze. He subjected the sleeper to his judgment and found it wanting.

I saw it all, though the door was closed, plain enough in my mind's eye. What passed between them was a discordance of cajolement and low threats, and dishonest senseless laughter. He struck Molly once, twice. I sat cross-legged with Squeaky in my lap and failed to get the creature to eat a single grain of boiled rice or a single flake of oatmeal.

Eventually, the man left, and I let myself out. I might have comforted her, but I didn't know how to approach her as she sat sobbing in the chair. She was far away at that moment, farther than my uncle was that night, farther than any human being could ever be from any other. I might have spread a blanket across her lap or brought a cup of water to her. But I didn't.

Pain creates a distance—a stretch of waste ground between one and the world; it is an exile.

A person gets bewildered there, runs out of water, is lured astray by voices. It is profane ground—vast, remote. There is no return from it until such time as the hurt person wills herself to recross the distance, suffers herself to be cared for again, and decides to forgive those whom she once trusted, those who went missing at the moment she needed them.

This decision to return is pain's only prerogative, and it may take years, lifetimes even, to choose it. There are many who get accustomed to those blinding distances. These will simply stay out there, away from everyone, and make a sort of life of it, but it isn't a happy life, because the only real insanity is loneliness, as many people know.

I have this vision of life. I've returned to it often over the years, and the passage of time only serves to confirm it. This vision transpires in a boundless tract of ocean. There, I see multitudes scattered across the face of the waters, clinging to broken spars, and I see many more treading water with no spar to cling to.

The fortunate ones agonize on the horns of a dilemma. Some paddle their broken spar towards the struggling ones, with the intention of offering some respite to a luckless soul caught in rough seas; they do this, even knowing they cannot prevent but only postpone their neighbor's demise, while pointlessly endangering themselves in the process.

But there are others among the fortunate who hug their spars, treading water in their charmed little circles of fear, keeping a hostile distance from the desperate and the drowning.

If the choice one makes in the face of this dilemma represents the only meaningful event in a person's life—as I believe it does—how bitter his existence must be to the one who chooses poorly.

We are all alike adrift, it's true, but it remains within my power to ease another's pain, if only for a moment. If I refuse to do that, I am a creature of no value. If I choose myself over others, I choose nothing at all. There are many possible truths concerning the purpose of life, and I've looked into a couple with more or less diligence. But as the years pass, they all fade under scrutiny. All but this one.

That evening, I had no idea what to do, and I missed my chance to comfort Molly. That is to say, I missed a costly opportunity. Not many such chances come along in the average life, and by declining even one, a person risks losing his soul and the whole world besides. I didn't console her, didn't so much as offer a drink of water, and I did not even come up with something to say.

She sat in silence in the chair for hours, leaning on her elbows, like a person tending a small fire that they may neither feed nor let die. Day turned to night and she lay down on the floor and wrapped herself in a blanket. In the morning, she resumed her seat, and watched the shadow slip beneath the juniper for hours. I set a cup of coffee beside her, but she left it untouched.

I was out in front of the sleeper, keeping Squeaky company. I'd staked out a little pen with chicken wire from Fargo's scrap heap. He'd given me a can of spinach, too, and I set a small leaf in an upturned seashell and placed it in the cage, but Squeaky was more intrigued by the tiny chips of quartz in the sand. It also ignored the crushed fleas I dropped at its toes. The soaring walls of its new cage caused more anxiety to me than to it, so I took Squeaky out and set it free to trip about in the sunshine. It was then that Molly stepped out, dressed in her green field jacket and carrying the satchel—the same with which she'd arrived.

She set the bag on the stoop, sat beside it, looked off toward the highway. I pretended not to notice, busying the moment with a search for fleas to set in Squeaky's erratic path. But the creature wouldn't eat.

Since the day of my uncle's death, I'd often wondered why Molly didn't leave the mesa and Santa Juana. I had no claims on her, nor she on me. If she wanted to depart, she needed only to tell Fargo or the police, and the law would see to a nine-year-old. There were established protocols for such matters: people who were obliged, by religion or the law or common charity, to look after an unaccompanied kid.

Time turned heavy, and I glanced up once to find her still seated— hands folded between her knees, leaning on her elbows—and looking directly at me with an expression I could not read. Her gaze passed through me and carried on, horizon by horizon. I turned back to the cage.

She stood, picked up the satchel, and went inside.

Far away, down in the valley, a freight trundled toward the skyline. The coal hoppers gleamed in the sun. The long train trembled like a live strand of wire.

After a few minutes, she opened the door and resumed her seat on the stoop, but barefoot now, with neither satchel nor jacket. She raked her hair back with her fingers, then took her brother's letter—still unopened—from her pocket.

For the first time in days, Molly spoke. She said my name, patted the board, and I sat beside her on the bottle crate stoop as she read her brother's letter to me.

Dear Molly,

I hope this letter finds you because I don't know where you are but I bet your not far from home. I got your letter thanks alot for that. I miss back there alot. . .

I still have the letter. It's been tucked into the pages of the Boyda Book for many years. The letter is written on government-issue stationary bearing a red eagle watermark at the top right corner: cheap paper that's no pleasure to write on. A few graphite thumbprints stain the margins where the writer held the letter between damp fingers.

Molly read on. As I listened to her voice, I pictured a man sitting on a stump in a forest of flowering trees. The man was young, to my mind, and wore a green helmet. He wrote on a notepad on his knee. Pink flowers drooped about him like so many smoky lamps. In my mind, the soldier had long red hair like Molly's. The tips of his hair touched the page as he composed, and the blue shadows of green leaves brushed the paper passingly.

You know what we found a huge black snake you wouldn't believe it how big. It was a beautiful animal and Sgt. vanden? put 15 rounds in it I was so mad stupid things like that happen sometimes here. Just boring though mostly really. Guess who I saw Benny Sandoval re-member from St. Pius he says hello. The weather is pretty beuatiful now but getting hotter by the day but right now is nice. Theres sun-sets that make me think of there. Give me New Mexico and a cold RC anyday! Im five months out not short but getting there. Please write again letters are a big deal really and I'll write to. Take care of yourself Molly the batteries in this flashlight are going out.

Tommy your brother

For several hours that day, and several the next, she drafted a response to her brother overseas, erasing phrases now and then, re-

reading passages, checking her thoughts against a wandering cloud or against his words, until she had covered six pages, printed front and back. Her handwriting was dense, pointed, precise—each letter plumb and square. The written page resembled the lines of a saga drafted in the original Icelandic—all tails and masts, hooks and beams.

After two days of writing, Molly sealed the envelope and said to me, Let's go to the post office, Ray Moon. I gotta send a letter to my brother.

She stood, brushed her pants, stretched her arms, tied her hair in a knot. She paused at the door to tend a passing thought.

He's clear across the whole dang world, she said. Can you believe it, Ray Moon?

Several days after Reginald Willie's first visit, just as I was finishing the Zuni history, the book truck roared up the track.

Molly dug a handful of coins from her jacket pocket, counted them twice, and told me to find four books. I picked out a World Book Encyclopedia, Volume *M*, a book called *Early Man in the Late Pleistocene*, an *Atlas of the Bible*, and one called *Stories from the Western Pueblos*. Molly picked out a book titled *Discovering the West* and one called *Dry Farmers' Almanac*. I returned the book we'd finished, and Molly paid the balance of a buck fifteen for the new purchases.

Molly invited Reginald Willie in for a lunch of bread and soup and black coffee. The book man cleaned his plate, extracted a toothpick from his wallet, thanked Molly, settled his cowboy hat on his head, and strode out into the sunshine with his shoulders back, humming a glad song.

That night I copied maps of Montana from the encyclopedia. The state was represented by various cartographic iterations of itself: on one map were the inkblots of lakes and clusters of triangles representing mountain ranges; another map displayed oil derricks, sheaves of wheat, and miniature factories dribbling curlicues of smoke. I copied them precisely on sheets of ruled paper and showed them to Molly, who praised them as women will and taped them to the wall with tabs of black electrical tape.

From the *Atlas* I copied the map of Saint Paul's journeys, a dashed line meandering from the Red Sea through Cilicia and Cappadocia, through Bithynia and Scythia. I made fair copies of Palestine under the Herods, the United Monarchy, and the Near East during the Assyrian Empire. I liked drawing maps because it took a lot of patience and concentration. And isn't it true that people are happiest when they have something to pay attention to? Attentiveness, someone said, is not godliness—it's God. I puzzled over that for years. But when I learned that the woman who'd said that had starved herself to death in despair at the suffering of others, I knew it must be true.

Molly and me studied our books. She opened *Discovering the West*, which turned out to be a history text for some high school in Denver. She read aloud the story of the Comanche leader Tavibo Naritgant, whom the Spaniards named Cuerno Verde—Green Horn—because he fastened a green-painted horn to his forehead during battle. For years, he raided the missions and the haciendas and stole horses and livestock until he was killed in an ambush. His green horn was presented to the viceroy of Nuevo Mexico, who gave it to the king, who gave it to the pope, and the visitor can find it there today, so the book said, in a gallery at the Vatican.

But the book didn't say why the pope would want to keep Tavibo Naritgant's green horn or display it in a case. The omission didn't trouble me much and I was prepared to turn the page. But Molly was not satisfied.

I heard the pope's palace is plated in gold, she said. So what's he need this horn for? I bet he sneaks down in his pointy slippers at night and puts that horn on. Can you see him, Ray Moon? Wearing pajamas and prancing about in that green horn, like some big kid in the dark?

She wiped her eyes.

If you ask me, she said, the pope oughtta give that green horn back. She turned the page.

There was a picture of Zebulon Pike wearing a rabbit-skin cap and a cape of muskrat pelts and a knee-length knife strapped to his hip. He was among the first Americans to visit this part of the world, and he was duly imprisoned in Santa Fe as a spy.

There was another picture of him, well-groomed and trussed-up in the high collar and gold braids of a Federal Army officer, bland as a man without a thought in his head. I'd have turned the page, but Molly lingered over the image, peering at it until, it seemed, Pike was compelled to speak up. In that portrait, he poses against a range of snowy mountains. That the scene was wholly contrived was a fact that Pike himself, under Molly's scrutiny, finally had to confess.

A lot of silliness found its way into that book, and though I had little knowledge to build on, I began to learn to read in the way Molly did—unhurried, meticulous, more or less forgiving. From her, I began to understand how a thing reveals its nature to the quiet observer but conceals its truths from distracted minds and passersby.

In the end, far from *Discovering the West* or anything else of value, Molly found only aggravation in this book, with its painted mountains and stolen horns and gold-braided imposters. She closed the book, handed it to me, and ordered me to bury it in the ground. So I did, in a shallow and unmarked grave, with a word of benediction—and a passing worry, too, for what Reginald Willie would say if he knew.

We set off on a walk in the desert and came upon a tarantula. Molly said, Oh, here's a science project for us.

The thing was sluggish because it was still early and cold. Molly shared an idea, and I ran back to the sleeper and returned with a metal dog dish and a scrap of pressboard. Molly scooped the spider gently into the dish, covered the dish with the board, and we started back. She set the thing free in the footless old washtub with the cracked glazing that sat in the perpetual shade of the sleeper's north wall.

We watched the spider for an hour, and it watched us. It only had to turn once to recognize the nature of its confinement; then it settled down to wait us out. A tarantula is smart, if patience is reckoned a form of intelligence—and patience may be the severest form of intelligence.

Molly read my thoughts.

This animal could teach us some things, Ray Moon, she said.

But as the tarantula's nature—its magnificent forbearance—revealed itself, it dawned on Molly that she'd committed a wrong. She coaxed the creature into the dish, carried it back to its home ground, and turned it loose.

It ambled off in its own time, ulterior to Molly's sincere regrets.

Having concluded the science project and noting the earliness of the hour, Molly remarked on the dead volcano—no more than an old rain-worn knob of a hill—that perched on the skyline. She decided to pack some bread and water and set off on a geological excursion. A two-hours' hike brought us to the volcano's precincts.

Encircling the low round cone was a broad skirt of lava that had fractured into interlocking columns. The polished, polygonal tops of these columns appeared, when viewed laterally, as a shattered lake of onyx. Each individual surface bore a dull gleam, like so many antique hand mirrors turned faceup to the sun—or a million stepping stones, each the width of one bare foot, and each set to a different height as to a different pitch.

As we stood looking across the lava rock, hoping to spy a way through, I noticed that one of these facets was wider and raised above the others, with a concave bowl on its sky-side. Inside the bowl were several stones—not pretty or otherwise notable, but smooth and clean as any stone from any riverbed in the world.

I looked about my feet and found a similarly unremarkable stone and dropped it in the bowl with the others.

▪

These days, I carry a pebble home from every walk in the city park and place the pebble in a glass jar on a shelf in my apartment. By now, the heavy jar strains the shelf brackets, and sometimes—on sleepless nights when I'm tired of reading—I take the jar down and reach in for a fistful and let them spill through my fingers. Somehow, the rocks never reach room temperature but retain the coolness of the inland seas they were buried in millions of years ago.

Human history sifts from time like sediment settles, self-burying, in a glass of water. The ways of people who lived long ago—their songs, their ceremonies, their works of art—are buried with the years in the strata of earth's memory. Like fragments of rare minerals, these will be unearthed, if not by a stubborn digger, then by the forces of winds and rivers on some distant unnumbered day.

All things—organic and inorganic—are bound to the rock cycle. Ossified, fossilized, metamorphosed: every mineral and shell—and every trace of human existence as well—is carried off in the perpetual round of burial and exposure, each according to its appointed hour on the geologic clock. The earth remembers, because it is a living ledger. In six billion years, it has discounted not so much as a fishbone, nor misplaced a pebble. It brings forth a little life for its moment in the sun, then bears it back into its depths again for a thousand years, or a hundred million years, as the case may be, according to its own undisclosed internal calculations. But there is this promise: nothing on earth exists but will—in similitude or paraphrase, though never unchanged—see many turns of light and darkness.

This cycle, however, does not assimilate acts of human violence with high efficiency. Anyone who has ever wandered alone, among the rocks and trees on a quiet evening, knows that some buried things have never been put to rest. *May the earth be light upon her bones* is an old blessing, one that reveals awareness of the trouble that arises when the proper rites are not attended to, or the dead are disrespected. The solitary walker, therefore, making their way through a place that has known unresolved pain, might sense an unsettled stirring beneath their shoes.

There are many such places in the world, where the restless unburied wander faint paths along dried-up streams, there to be glimpsed on occasion by the living—by the poor in spirit, or by children, or fugitives, or those disposed to solitude. Nevertheless, even these—even if they stop and shield their eyes and strain to peer through the too-bright light or blowing dust at something moving in the distance—are never quite certain what it is they see.

When Cain slew Abel, it's said, the blood cried out from the ground. This is no metaphor, no figure of speech to anyone who has ever walked at the edge of the dark, when evening pours from its artesian springs and overspills the canyons.

The dead linger and have reasons to do so. Many of them merely wish to draw the living to themselves, in the hopes of alleviating the awful loneliness that is (according to some testimonies) elemental to the afterlife. Others, however, harbor the wish to harm those who harmed them, or to inflict trouble on the descendants of the killers and tormenters, the slavers or thieves.

The mountains, I should add, are the sentinels of the cycles; they testify to the land's memorial power. On clear breezy days, in the high deserts, the mountains seem not to encumber the earth at all—appear weightless, in fact, borne a handbreadth above the horizon on a thin bed of dust. Burdens neither to the land nor to those asleep beneath the ground, they offer testimony that what is buried is, for good or ill, not buried forever.

❧

It was in the stories I borrowed from Reginald Willie's truck that I learned how the dead return to water the fields, or that they sleep—dry as cornstalks—in the cliff towns to this day.

Furthermore, the dead guard the lightning flashes, the books affirmed, and carry just-enough rain in hand-painted funerary bowls. And in spring, the trees shake loose clouds of pollen that are the life-sustaining breath of the underworld (or of the next world, or the other world, depending on who's telling the story).

These bits of knowledge confirmed or contradicted each other, for they came from different peoples and from different times, but together they constituted a firmament of truths—each story discrete, unique, but redolent of the same soil.

Had I the faith of a mustard seed, I would believe them all. I would understand them clearly, because faith is merely the prelude to understanding. *Credo ut intelligam*—I believe, that I might understand. Saint Anselm said that a thousand years ago. Such faith is difficult; it fades fast in this world.

There is something wrong with my eyes, no doubt. I just don't have the heart to see things as they really are. Perhaps it is better for a timid, nowaday creature like me to whistle past these hard matters because, as any reasonable citizen knows, a spirit cannot be seen. It cannot be encountered on a bus or in a checkout line. It cannot be met on an empty street one early Sunday morning in your hometown.

Everybody knows that.

I was speaking of the dead volcano.

Upon placing the unremarkable stone into the stone bowl, I realized that Molly was no longer with me. Perhaps she was investigating a lizard, I thought, somewhere back along the way.

Halfway to the volcano's base, after an hour of hop-stepping the lava stones, I came upon a vent in the earth. I climbed down and entered a rounded chamber with a smooth sandy floor.

Across the walls, at shoulder-height, were chiseled images: a quaver note within a hazard triangle; three jars covered by a roof; a deer tick feeding on the sun.

A girl balanced on one leg, at the end of a plank.

A scorpion like a burnt guitar.

An unfinished game of hangman. Helicopters in a V like a flight of geese. A yellow-eyed monster.

A fire rake, a helix, a sun with three spots, and many other figures or symbols I could not name.

These chiseled images proceeded laterally across the wall, quiet as moons, or the way one's thoughts revolve in a sleepless dark.

A woman entered. I hid myself in a crevice in the wall. With her back to me, she sat cross-legged on the ground and extracted a hummingbird's nest from a pouch. With the nest for tinder, she kindled a fire, and the fire limned her shoulders with gold light as she fed the flames, twig by twig.

She did not move, I could not escape, and it grew cold in the shadows. Minutes turned to hours. Another woman, thin and gray, entered the cave bearing an oil lamp of clay. She sat across from the younger woman, set the lamp aside, and extinguished the flame with thumb and finger. After they had each fed a stick to the fire, the younger woman spoke.

"I'm glad to see you, mother. You've put out the flame. Has it come to that?"

"I'm glad to see you, daughter. There is no oil to be had on the wide earth. I will keep searching."

"And when it's all gone? What then?"

"What then? They'll forget the days, then the words, then the way back."

"And what will become of us?"

"We'll go dark. Just like them."

The older woman held her palms to the flame, rubbed her hands.

"Are you tired, mother?"

"I am."

"Go and rest. What is it, mother?"

"It was a good day, all in all."

"I'm glad. What is it, mother?"

"There's something else here with us."

"That's so. What is it?"

"A child."

"Frightened?"

"Petrified."

"Hm. The young are always in trouble," said the younger woman. "Is it an intelligent child?"

"Not really."

"I see. Go rest, please, mother. Good night, and thank you."

The older woman lit the lamp with a burning twig and departed.

"Misfortunate child, sit here," the woman said, and I emerged from my hiding place and sat beside the fire. She wore a faded blue shawl and a coronal of dried roses. A plain cotton mask was pressed like a bandage to her face, cleaved in place with blood. The fabric shone darkly where fresh blood had seeped through the dried. Three holes—one for her mouth and two for her eyes—gleamed like rain-slick rock.

"Do you know what I am?" she asked.

"No."

"Do you believe everything you're told?"

"I don't know."

"Where are you going?"

"Nowhere—I'm just out wandering."

"Wandering? Since you've disturbed this place with your wandering," she said, "it's going to be more difficult to arrive where you're going. You could have kept your eyes and ears shut, like reasonable people do, and saved trouble. Now you have to start at the beginning."

"Where am I going?"

She lifted her face to the cave's roof, and so did I. The chiseled images proceeded in counterclockwise file about the rounded chamber of the cave, ascending as they revolved about us; row on row, they climbed in a low-pitch spiral. The spiral accelerated and narrowed as it neared the apex of the cave, and there, one by one, the chiseled images drained into a black hole.

The woman dwelt on the whirling firmament for a moment, then turned to me. "Seven times you'll return. Each time, you'll find yourself a little nearer to your destination. The eighth time you'll arrive. To go forward, you must go back. Understand? That's it, boy. That's all there is."

"Arrive where? I don't want to arrive anywhere, ma'am."

"Then you should not have placed the stone with the stones. Now it's too late." She added a stick to the flames. "For that, I'm going to make you take the long way round, and take it wide awake. If you want to live, keep your eyes and ears open and your mouth shut."

"Why seven times?"

"I shouldn't have to explain."

The flames died; the chiseled images faded. "But where am I going?"

"How would I know?"

"Who are you?"

"The daughter of memory. Who are you?"

I woke up in the sleeper and walked into the kitchen to find a bowl of soup on the table.

Are you hungry? Molly asked.

I sat, took a stone out of my pocket, and set it beside the soup bowl so I could examine the thing as I ate.

The room shivered and ticked. Great orange combers of wind, saturated with static energy, broke over the sleeper, causing it to shake on its blocks. The wind gnawed at holes the size of needles' eyes and filled my mind with blue whistles.

When Molly's back was turned, I slid open the window and tossed the stone away.

Molly decided to go to town.

Ray Moon, she said. Them men gave us a lot of money the day they buried Edward. Do you think they'd mind if we bought sandwiches with that money?

I don't think so, Molly.

So we got in the truck, which Fargo had towed home and repaired for nothing. But now the truck was out of gas. Molly fetched the fuel can and held it like a basketball to her ear, shook it once, and listened for a slosh.

There's a couple miles in this thing yet, Ray Moon, she said.

I made a funnel out of newspaper and slipped it in the filler neck and Molly poured the gas in, joggling the final drops free. She set the can aside, squatted in the sand, turned me by the elbows so that I faced her. She smoothed my hair with gasoline fingers, fussed my jacket.

Hm. I think you need to wash up a bit, Ray Moon.

She filled a stainless steel dog bowl with water and dipped a rag and scrubbed behind my ears.

Do your fingers, she said, and teased me. Look what happened to you! All a sudden you're a handsome boy. Let's go.

We drove to town and ordered two egg sandwiches at the diner. As the nice lady prepared our food, she paused and sniffed about. Do you smell gasoline? she asked Molly.

Yes, I do, Molly said, sniffing helpfully. We drove here in a truck.

Here you are, daughter, the woman said. You don't want to eat in here?

No ma'am! Thank you!

Molly was so happy to buy a sandwich after weeks of oatmeal and canned soup, she sang a song about a woman in a barroom and a man who's unhappy about it.

She held my hand as we hurried down the cold afternoon sidewalks. Curtains of dust blew up the street. Tammy Wynette it was—the song Molly sang, I mean. Tammy Wynette's songs played on many radios in that place in those years, and not a few people knew all the words to every tune.

●

At a dead fountain at a deserted corner, we sat and ate the sandwiches. Molly admired the stone angel perched on the dry pipe, yearning bare-armed at the sky.

Ah. Look, Ray Moon. She has wings. Do you wish you had wings?

I never thought about it, Molly.

If I had wings, she said, I'd fly everywhere! I'd go see that big waterspout that spouts outta the ground all the time. Or that big tree people drive their cars right through.

Where's that at?

Hm. Probably they're not in the same place.

We laughed at that and didn't know why.

She thought a moment and continued more solemnly. If I had wings, man, I'd go to Albuquerque, she said. I'd fly to Albuquerque to my uncle's house who owes me forty dollars. Dang! If I had wings I'd fly down and get my forty dollars, then buy us some steaks and green beans at the K-Bar Steak House.

She wiped my mouth with a napkin, then wiped her own.

We ate fast, alert to everything.

And while I'm there, she added grimly, maybe I'll fly by his windows a few times. Just to scare him.

Who?

My uncle, dummy! Don't you listen, boy? We should come to town more often, Ray Moon, she said. It's not so dirty as some towns.

I had not visited town very often. Once, my uncle brought me to the Santa Juana Bike & Hobby Shop. After he had scorned the new bikes, the proprietor led us to the used ones that were huddled like a brace of starved goats in the corner. My uncle and the man argued over a black Huffy.

I'm not paying no twenty dollars, my uncle had stated. You know why? I don't have twenty dollars. This bike is used, man. Used means used. Take twelve.

That was a good day. The man gave us the bike for thirteen dollars and I rode it for weeks.

Sitting together at the fountain, I told Molly the whole story about the visit to the Bike & Hobby Shop.

That's a good story, boy, she said to me. Where's that bike at now?

I left it lying in the lane, I said, and he drove over it in the dark in his truck. I felt gratified hearing Molly laugh so free and loud.

That truck's always been an ill-omened thing, she said.

✤

We were sitting on the lip of the dry fountain, content to savor the meal and watch the scant traffic, when a man on a bike pulled to a stop in front of us. His bicycle was laden fore and aft: a backpack was fastened to the rack behind his seat, and a stained cloth sack hung from the handlebars. A transistor radio was strapped to the crossbar with electrical tape. The bike's owner wore a denim cap that read Boilermakers #39, a shoe wrapped in electrical tape that resembled a primitive moonboot, and one of those beards men grow in forests.

It's Tuesday, he said.

Molly looked up and down and around and reached for my hand. It is Tuesday, she repeated, but her words carried less conviction than his.

The pantry's open today, the man said. Bag a food for free at Saint Alban's. Tuesdays only. Good stuff, too, lady. Chef Boyardee and Spam. Beans and tortillas and stuff. Maybe canned chicken if you're lucky. Corn, who knows! Right over there. At that little church. See it? They open in about ten minutes.

Okay. Thank you.

Don't thank me, it aint my food, he said, and peered closer at the two of us. What's the matter? Cops after you?

Cops! Ha! She glanced at me. I don't think so, she said.

They probably are, though, the man informed us. You just don't know it. Me and you, he said to Molly, we don't look right. For example, I'm missing several teeth, and you're wearing shower shoes. And you got a kid with you who don't resemble you, which raises a number of difficult questions. Yeah, they're probably watching you right now, right this minute.

Molly looked up and down the street and checked the sky for good measure.

What's your street name?

My street name? It's Molly.

No, not your real name. Your street name. You need a street name so they can't so easily find you. Get one for the boy, too.

Molly looked at me and said, I like my name but okay. You're probably right.

I am right, but suit yourself. My name's P.D.

He held his hand out, and Molly took it. He told us he'd been riding his bike for three years. His hand testified to the truth of this: its knuckles hatched with starshaped cracks, the legacy of frostbit nights and table wine.

His bike was a battlewagon. The tires were worn to fuzz where they met pavement, and the frame was held together by a few spot welds and some lucky grease stains.

What's your name? he asked me.

Raymond.

There's a war coming, Raymond. Not this little brushfire going on now in Viet Nam, I mean the real thing. It's gonna come like a thief in the night, like the good book says, and you'll either be ready or you won't. Me? I got caches of food in thirty-four places between here and Cruces and I got maps for each cache written in hieroglyphics that only I can cipher. Look. You can see for yourself.

He opened his jacket revealing a leather pouch, creased and stained as though it had been carried for years on the Flagstaff-Kingman express. From the pouch he extracted a sheet of paper and brandished it at us like a confession wanting a signature.

On the paper were puddles of dots, a few transmission towers resembling scaffolds, and meandering dashed lines that may have signified dry creek beds. There was a mysterious image of two stick figures beneath a pitched roof, like a Chinese thought-picture of tranquility. A few inches from this image was a black cross, and connecting the two was a straight line underscoring the number *188*.

I took immense joy in examining P.D.'s map. It was intricate, beautiful, crafted with pain and care, and resembled, in my memory's eye, a schematic for a futuristic hay rake, or an ancient star chart from the days when the sky was alive. P.D. waited and watched while I strained to make sense of it. I handed it over, at a loss for the proper word of praise, and he tucked it tenderly away.

Molly wasn't so nervous anymore because, even though the man was dusty and starved, he had shared with us these important matters of food caches and the coming war. It felt conspiratorial, like he'd taken one look at her and admitted her to his whatnot of a secret society. I doubt Molly had ever belonged to a society, so she warmed to him.

The man was out of his mind and nice. You can be both. Not everyone can accept that.

P.D. told us he'd gotten kicked out of a famous university—I forget the name. This is what he said: They called me in and told me I wasn't making satisfactory progress toward a degree so I said look here you silly sonsabitches I'm making satisfactory progress toward three goddamn degrees so they yanked my deferment and packed me off to a jungle but now I'm back and living off forty cents a day. Forty cents a day. I know every pantry between Tucson and Tucumcari. Ever drink your own pee? I'll show you how it's done. It'll take a few years before you become as proficient as me, though.

He pointed vaguely beyond the highway.

I'm gonna cache today's food out there, he said. We're surrounded by public range land. Did you know that? Sixty thousand acres and it's all mine! Yours, too, lady. Water aint a problem neither. In this state, it's against the law to refuse anyone a drink a water. Do you believe me?

I'm sorry, Molly said. Would you repeat that?

A radio program, P.D. said. It's called *Salt of the Earth*. We have music, news, and helpful information. It's in the building with the big antenna, next to the tire shop. Somebody told me the president of the united-goddamn-states tunes in to my program on occasion. What happens is, I complain about some things, then I play some family music, then I move on to survival skills. That's it. You can be in on it, too, if you like. Maybe you could read the public service announcements. It's a federal thing, you know. The kid can help. Whatta you say, kid? Wanna be a radio personality?

Yes.

Molly looked at me like I'd summoned a demon.

Good! the man said. Why don't you bring a poem to read? That would add a touch of class to the show. Specially if a woman reads it. Be at the station in two days, Saturday, ten in the morning.

He pedaled off and Molly groaned at the sky, then stiffened at a thought. Ray Moon, she said, I never talked on a radio. Won't that be fun! Will you help me write a poem?

You don't have to go, Molly. I said. Why not just not show up? I don't think he's normal so it's okay.

She considered then rejected that option.

No, she said, as we turned down the street. It's always best to be nice to crazy people, Ray Moon. You might need their help some day.

That afternoon, we inventoried the windfall from Saint Alban's pantry: a pack of hot dogs and two tins of Spam, a sack of potatoes, five cans of diced peppers, three of white beans, one of sliced pineapple, a loaf of bread, two pounds of rice.

After putting the food away, I changed Squeaky's water, and let it trip free for a time outside its cage. I followed behind as it made its way from pebble to twig, from stick to stone, erringly toward the mesa's edge, where the low sun waited.

I wondered what Squeaky thought of me, a Goon Colossus bumbling along with my fat hands and moon face, a thoughtless monster blotting the sky. In proportion to Squeaky I was the size of a five-story building, unmoored from its foundation. But this did not trouble the chick. My capacity for harm, as the creature surely knew, was hopelessly misoriented, and for this reason Squeaky accepted my company without conditions as we made our crooked ways sunward.

Having considered its smallness in relation to me, I further considered my own insignificance in relation to the sun, now a tipped red pitcher at sundown, spilling green clouds across the western sky.

Because childhood has difficulty discerning the ends of things, I tinkered with the possibility that there was another Being who, unbeknownst to me, drifted hugely through this sky, like one of those enormous fiddlers who hover over impoverished Russian villages—a Being as mindful of my movements as I was of Squeaky's.

As I followed the chick, I counted myself a trifle on this earth.

It shouldn't be wondered that I was visited by such thoughts because, while it is true that childhood is rich in marvels, it's also a melancholy season. To the child's mind, the earth reveals its immensity, and the sky reveals its indifference at an early age, often simultaneously. A child soon understands that stars appear and fade regardless of his wishes, and he begins to suspect that the masters of life—whatever they may be—are preoccupied with issues infinitely larger than himself.

How was it, then, that Squeaky could be the source of such desperate worry on my part?

We arrived at the edge of the mesa. Silence shot across the sky like a star.

At the appointed hour, we arrived at the radio station, the only building with an antenna on top. But the station was locked and boarded. CLOSED, read the yellow notice, BY ORDER OF THE SANTA JUANA COUNTY COMMISSION.

Molly and me cupped our hands at the grimy pane and peered inside. In the middle of the littered floor sat a three-legged stool. Wires dangled from the ceiling like dead vines. A voice, smooth and deep, startled me.

The mayor's a friend of mine. Bobby Sanchez.

We turned to see the sheriff standing behind us, one thumb hooked into his Sam Browne, revolver hanging slack at his hip. The bright sun behind his shoulder carved him into silhouette.

Never heard of him, Molly said.

Bobby Sanchez, the mayor. He owns this place. Some hobo was in here, playin with the old busted up radio equipment. I bet he invited you on his famous radio program, didn't he? You wouldn't be the first.

Molly's face set as the man turned his head and spat. She took me by the elbow and said, We gotta go.

But you aint heard the story, the sheriff said, with a step in her direction that made her stop and tighten her grip.

See, that hobo set up the microphone and spliced a few wires and pretended he was running a real-life radio program like a modern-day Baby Snooks. You could stand right here and watch him preachin his Gospel of Saint Goofball, as Bobby called it. But that hobo's voice never traveled far, cause Bobby, you see, he'd turned that transmitter off long ago. He didn't tell your friend, though. He even charged that hobo two dollars, which he paid in pennies and nickels, on time, every first of the month. He was prompt, that fella—what's his name? Yep, that Bobby Sanchez has got him a funny sense a humor. The only creatures who listen to that hobo are the mice that live in the walls. There's no harm in it, I guess.

The sheriff chuckled, turned, and spat.

Good-bye, Molly said, leading me away by the elbow.

A lot a druggies running around these days, talking crazy talk, the sheriff said as we walked away. I worry about you, Molly, all alone up there. I'll be by to check on you.

No, don't do that, she called over her shoulder. No need.

We struck a steady pace, by devious directions, following arroyos far into the desert. Out of sight of the town, Molly sat in the cool, gin-laced shade of a juniper and composed a poem for P.D.'s radio program. The program's nonexistence did not acquit her of the promise. When she had finished, she read it for me.

Fifty years on, I remember it perfectly, as I remember most things. Here it is, in its unabridged entirety:

> If I had a pair a wings
> I'd fly to Albuquerque with the ducks
> And make my lazy no good uncle
> Pay me back my forty bucks.

With the pencil and paper in her lap, Molly dozed, cradled in the juniper's roots as in the bony fingers of a hand. So I set off on a wander, toward the only cloud in the whole wide round of the sky. From the cloud trailed three thin gray ribbons of rain, which fell like a sifting of ash upon a hill.

On the way toward that rain, I was stopped by a sound. Coyotes, I first thought, and walked on, but the cries grew louder, and assumed a human timbre. I crept to the head of an arroyo and peered over the lip. There, in a dry shallow streambed, was a man on his knees, stripped to the waist, rubbing his arms with handfuls of sand. Dust trickled from his neck like water.

It was P.D. Rinsed with dust, he climbed to his feet and spoke—to the stones, to the vanished waters, to no one I could see. He catechized the cactus wrens and the thrashers that flitted among the tamarisks. Questions, questions wrapped in pleas, pleas salted with stark imprecations.

Though I could neither distinguish nor understand the words, I have come to recognize the voice. It is the voice of the clay accusing the potter, the common greek of banished people. It's not a seldom voice, these days: you hear it in the city, beside the highway, in the waste ground at the edges of towns. An immemorial idiom that survives, and will always survive, among the exiled.

I slipped back down and took another way toward the cloud.

As I walked, the land changed. The dusty earth became gravel and sand laid in long gray wind-rippled beds that wended toward the skyline. Nothing moved but a few shreds of fog. The sun was a silver core drilled at the apex of a sulfur-yellow sky.

The stony land inclined to a crest, and there I stopped. From the edge, the cliff plunged sheer into a sea of mist that pulsed with green thunderlight. The depths rumbled, exhaling rime. I peered over and let the rising air, bitter as the draft from a doused furnace, wash over my face.

A powerful wind divided the mist, then, revealing land. Now visible on the plain were immense copper-colored, water-carven spires of stone. As the mists rolled, revealing more land, braided red rivers in shallow beds appeared.

By now, the wind had swept the entire plain clean. In the middle distance squatted a brace of volcanoes, heaving ash like a fleet of dreadnoughts under steam. The slopes of one volcano were streaked with livid streams of lava that resembled the hairline seams on a skull.

A few electrified thunderheads, dragging torn shrouds of rain, stalked that stone wilderness. And trimming the skyline like a blade was the great blue gleaming wall of ice. The earth sagged, it seemed, if only by inches, beneath the weight of the glacier. Before the million sun-faceted eyes of the ice, scarlet tornadoes spun like colossal rock-drills, casting up storms of dust.

In the foreground, tiny and black, several figures were on the move, in file, across the vastity. Animal or human, I couldn't say.

The end of the world exists. It's a true place. At the cliff's edge, abyssal winds trick runnels of dust from the lip that vanish as they spill. You can stand at the edge and feel it erode beneath the soles of your shoes. You can taste the dead seas in the roots of your teeth.

✤

The mists regathered, obscuring the scene. I turned back, where the familiar sun shone again on the familiar land. It's well, I thought, to watch where I put my feet, and pay close attention at all times to what I was about, because the world is filled with half-open doors that open on unattended passages that lead to god-knows-where. If I'm not careful, I thought, I'll find the next door has shut behind me.

When I reached the sleeper, I found Molly on the shady side, scratching in the hard earth with a hoe. She straightened, wiped the sweat from her eyes, and cast a critical glance back over the three low mounds of earth.

What are you doing, Molly?

We're gonna make a garden, boy.

Will things grow here?

Fargo said they might, though it aint the best place, and it's late to
be starting. All and all, we oughtta grow some food for ourselves. This
is the world we live in, Ray Moon. We keep our eyes and ears open and
our mouths shut. Maybe we'll learn something.

Molly?

What is it?

. . . never mind.

Beside the sleeper was a wicker basket fitted with shoulder straps.
She asked me to try it on.

Now off you go, she said.

Where should I go, Molly?

You're the fertilizer boy! Go on down to the desert and follow Fargo's horses and fill that basket with horse pats. Not the wet kind, but
the dry kind. Medium well is okay too, she said. That's Fargo's basket
so don't bust it. Now git!

And with that she turned back to her work.

It didn't take long to track down a few dozen dry pats. I returned
within an hour, proud to spill my haul of manure on the ground like a
draft of fish. Molly praised the catch. She dug up the baby jar that contained the firemen's money, unrolled a few bills, handed them to me,
and we walked to town. With five dollars tucked under my hat, I
stepped into the feed-and-seed shop like a landowner.

When you put all the seeds in the world in one room, each in their
proper bins, and add some chicks and poults, and a few baskets of bird
seed, and big troughs of mast for pigs, the mix is head-lightening,
sweeter than a field of poppies. While I was burying my hands in a bin
of hayseed, marveling at the silky coolness of it, Molly was very meticu-
lously dropping beans into a small paper envelope.

We paid for our goods and set off for the sleeper. From the pockets
of Molly's government issue jacket protruded the silky tufts of corn in
the husk, like a passel of tousled little children.

All day, we turned the manure with the soil until it softened, turning and turning. I made a few trips to the desert to collect dung and some soft soil from the banks of a dry streambed, and humped these back to Molly.

Fargo arrived after dinner with a coil of bare wire and several stakes, which he drove in around the garden with a hand sledge. He ran the wire from stake to stake, then connected the wire to the posts of a pair of car batteries.

Now pretend you're a rabbit, kid, and stick your little paw on the wire, he said.

I did so, and for my trouble I received a jolt that I could taste.

That's rabbit wire, son, Fargo said. It only shocks rabbits. Is there anything you'd like to tell us?

I wonder if there's a little white tail under them trousers, Molly said, laughing to the skies.

Their ridicule made my eyes burn, and I shouldered the dung basket and set off, the anger churning in my gut. Their entreaties to turn back were lost to the ringing in my ears.

Night fell as I wandered, my thumbs hitched in the straps. The weight of the basket was a comfort, more so because I put nothing into it. I can't say how it was, but that empty basket gave me a license to travel, and I found myself in a place I'd never been before.

Stars resolved, like crystals in a rinsed dish, brightening as the day's shores went dark. It was with the stars in my mind that I came to a lookout stone.

Below was a shallow bowl of green land rimmed by low chains of mountains. In the middle of the bowl was a town built like a house of cards, but stouter. Scattered small windows glowed with the flickering pink of interior fires.

Wide paved roads, running true as crow flight, radiated from the town in five directions, and disappeared over each horizon. These roads were punctuated at intervals by blazing torches, and along them went many people, returning or setting forth, singly or in pairs or in small parties. Some shouldered baskets; some carried infants; some went freehanded and unhurried, attended by laughter and song. The sound of happy voices carried plainly to my ears, amplified in the dust-less air, with the clarity of sound over water. The full moon rose and took an interest, it seemed, in the comings and goings of the people; it settled back in its wonted balcony above the eastern mountains and held the good creatures of the earth in its old benevolent regard.

Now, the moon's true form escapes the naked eye. Through a tele-scope you can see how shadows rake the lunar seas, and you might infer therefrom its roundness. But it looks flat to most eyes on most nights.

But this night was different. The last light died, the roads cleared, and the change came over the moon.

On its eastern hemisphere, there commenced a low burn like a shortgrass fire. I slipped off the basket and sat down to watch the smol-der spread across the moon's face, which changed color from bone-white to livid. As the burn spread to consume the last west corner, the moon revealed its true mass—rich and round as too-ripe fruit, pend-ing low above the earth. Imminent it was now, lambent as blood.

A tumult rose from the darkened town, the sound of a vast orches-tra tuning up: horns and drums and pipes, shouts and whistles, rattles and brassy gongs. Placated by all that happy noise, the fever did grad-ually cool and fade, and the moon resumed his pale and placid vigil.

I returned to the sleeper after dark.

❧

The next evening, I set out a dish of water with a few flakes of oat-meal in it, but Squeaky preferred to peck at the dirt. As the chick peeped and kept on starving, Molly sat on a stool beside the garden, deep in a brown study of the corn seed germinating beneath the small mounds of soil.

After a time, I gathered Squeaky up and let it fuss in my lap as we sat on the ground at Molly's feet. The clouds, the sun, and the sky attended her thoughts, it seemed, as she communed with the little life strug-gling under the ground.

On that evening, as I sat at Molly's knee watching the mountains, a suspicion began to stir, a suspicion that has, from that moment, colored my understanding. It was this: any given mountain is never the same from one year to the next, or from one day to the next, or from one minute to the next.

I didn't know how it could be that such a self-evident fact had for so long eluded me. There's a Chinese saying about singing to the ox, and I suspect that, like the ox, I had no comprehension of the marvels that beset me.

The shadow-pattern on the mountains, I realized, is always different because the sun is always moving; and the next day at the same time the shadow-pattern will be different again—all meteorological factors being equal—because the sun will be on a new and different transit, some fraction of a degree off yesterday's. And over the coming years, as I began to grasp the structure of our solar system, I understood that the pattern of shadow and light on the land won't be the same a year from today, because by then the earth will have veered a bit in its orbit, and this year's angle—that is, of the earth relative to the sun—will be lost for maybe a million years, maybe forever. And even if the earth didn't veer, the light would still be different a year from now, because the mountain will have been worn down by the works of wind and rain. Furthermore, even if *all this* were not true, the brightness of the sun does change by the hour—affecting our perceptions of things like mountains—for it is dying as you read this, and is in fact turning brighter, not dimmer, as it dies.

This truth—about the changefulness of the world—was sown in watchfulness. Its implications would be years in sinking roots. It has still not borne fruit of any worth.

Ancient Greeks were troubled by the fact of mutability, as their plays and poems show. More so, at any rate, than their medieval inheritors with their golden chains and *scala naturae*. For centuries, Greek thinkers sought for a patch of dry land in reason's perilous seas, a place from which to cast one irrefutable reading of the sky.

Ignorant of Moses, they did not inhabit a world created once for all in a week. They knew that mountains rise and fall, for they lived in a mountainous land (and a volcanic one, too) where entire islands had been known to vanish (which made for splendid stories).

Change. Many letters for a single syllable: *change*. There's a talismanic chime to it. It lends itself to hexes. I believe it's from the French.

Change, for the Greeks, was the one irreducible fact, and for this reason the essential nature of existence was an ungraspable thing. Every Aegean voyage, for example, took place under the bemused eyes of Proteus, the shape-shifter, perched high atop some startling wave-beaten rock. To achieve a measure of serenity in the cosmic flux was an act of courage and wisdom, an act as rare then as now. It was only the things that did *not* change—man's incorrigible nature, above all—that gave legitimate reason to despair.

There was a poet. He suspected the presence of a more durable reality, one situated beyond mere appearances, inaccessible to the bodily senses. There is another mountain, this poet said, that exists in the heavens, and this mountain has always been, and it will always be, and it will never change or erupt or sink. Wind and rain, he said, will never wear it away.

Not only the mountain. Every single thing that apparently passes into and out of existence, he said, has its eternal counterpart. Chrysanthemums and friendships and foxes: all of these are but emanations of originals that reside in the eternal mind, where they prevail, inviolably and everlastingly.

These originals he called ideas, and these ideas constitute the matrices of all knowledge. They are planted like seeds in an individual's mind from birth. The soul, as well, has its corresponding idea, and this is known as Truth, or Beauty. Another thinker—the poet's compatriot—pondering similar problems, likened the soul in its body to a spider in its web, which is a lovely image for another day.

These seeds of knowledge may grow into flowers of knowledge, or trees of understanding, but they must be cultivated in full awareness that all of sensible life is ephemeral, and that its passage is brief and filled with confusion and trouble. These seeds must be watered, as well, by love—love for mortal and transient creatures that, like our-selves, participate in the truths that they reflect, and are sacred for that reason.

Every single thing in the wide earth emerges from nothing and dissolves into nothing again. The testimony of the senses affirms it. This plain fact has led at least one puzzled creature, in each of the last five hundred generations of human beings, to ask, *What is real?*

How comforting, then, this new philosophy of ideas, or forms, must have been to those who, at last, had found that one fixed and permanent place—that one patch of dry and stable ground—on which to plant their feet and look about and say out loud, against all the evidence of their eyes and ears: *This* is true, and *Here* endures.

Now, to accept the transitory nature of earthly things, and to love them despite—or because of—the brevity of their passage, is wisdom, and wisdom is difficult. But it's more difficult to love what does not pass away, for there is something eerie and unnatural about such things.

I don't know what inspired the ancient poet to devise his ideal kingdom. That world of enduring forms, I suspect, was a place where he hoped to evade the erosions of Time, or to find even a shred of meaning in the flux. But he only succeeded in trading the prison of eventfulness for the prison of nonevent.

The man who devised this system was beloved by his medieval inheritors. To their minds, he had established a rational basis for that weird proclivity, peculiar to human beings, to believe in the unseen—that malarial delirium called faith. Of course, he intended no such thing.

Any child today would understand, if you explained it to them, what the poet was after. Every child inhabits a like domain, more or less sophisticated than the Greek's. It's said that the imaginative power fades with age, and that's true enough. To speak more precisely, though, it may be better to say that the child's gift lies not in a capacity for more vivid fantasies, but in the ability to pass freely between this mortal world and that shadowless preexistence—the first home of the soul—where the prototypes of all things drift unencumbered by decay. It is the conscience of the grown man—conscience burdened with guilt—that prevents him from entering that place, and so he chooses, with the injured pride of the excluded, to deride and deny its very existence. He may even fool himself now and then, and his mockery, in time, calcifies into character, and disbelief becomes a self-fulfilling prophecy. In the end, however, it is not eternity that is rejected, but oneself. Age will only confirm the banishment that pride incurred. The end will be bitter for such a one, littered with discarded illusions. Anyway, it's an old story.

This much I know. Every coyote and bird I encountered during those walks with Molly seemed to have just arrived from that very eternity, and they never failed to share its news. So near it was—that other world, beside us all the while—so near it was, a breeze from there could make my hair stand on end.

To *believe in* someone or in some thing: it means, I think, to acknowledge that a given creature is possessed of some quality that is lasting, indestructible—something that will persist even after that creature has ceased to be. To believe in someone is to believe that there is, at the inmost core of every being, some element that death is powerless to extinguish.

Molly believed in the world, in tumbleweeds and clouds. Untutored, she intuited the old philosophy of forms I've been jabbering on about. She believed in this world, and in the intrinsic worth of every stone and bird. I contracted that faith like a virus from which, in the coming years, I'd recover at times. But the fever always returns, recurring even still to afflict me with inklings of a presence—call it love, call it god—that is mindful, in some small way, of every earthly thing.

All things and all people were real to Molly, and she believed in them implicitly.

All things, that is, with the exception of herself.

She stepped lightly through this world, therefore, knowing she would not escape or belong, and she made a home in a place too dry and too remote to be coveted by many others.

And guessing that I was lonely like her, she made a home there for me as well.

⚊

We went for a walk in the desert—in the days after the planting but before the first sprout. Molly brought along the Boyda Book and, on a blank back page, she began a catalogue of stones.

The *Swan Skull* was a stone the size of a walnut: skull-shaped; its eye sockets packed with copper-colored dust; the bill smooth and sealed shut. As such it was entered into the book, along with a brief description—a task she delegated to me—and the location and the hour of discovery.

A knuckle of sandstone shot with perfect holes on its eastern hemisphere, where an ancient colony of worms once lived, she named *Worm Stone*.

A core of arrow-stone, whose every facet was the shape of an arrowhead, she christened *Hunting Stone*.

A stone, split to reveal a pink interior flaked with crystal, was the *Grapefruit Stone*.

About noon, as we climbed out of an arroyo into the open air, Molly paused and peered into the distance, one hand shading her eyes.

Look, Ray Moon, she said. There's green trees up on that mountain.

I did not at first see what Molly saw. Before that day, I hadn't noticed any trees in that direction.

I stood beside Molly and followed her finger and, true enough, there was a brief irruption of green like a low flame edging the crest. A careless glance would have revealed only a cloud setting on the mountain's blind side, or a trick of the eye.

We returned to the sleeper and packed the satchel with a bottle of water and a loaf of bread, donned our hats and coats, and set off. After an hour's walk, the mesa was far behind us, but the trees we sought had drawn hardly nearer.

At last we came to the foot of the mountain. As we ascended, we

passed outcrops of silver rock like the horsehair crests on Trojan helmets. Ravens and swallows, and other birds we did not know, had made
their homes, their way stations, or their observation posts in those
high places. Crows rode the converging winds in mazy gusts, ill-
disciplined as blowing leaves. Their calls ricocheted in the stillness.

While we sat on a flat rock and shared a drink of water, a golden
eagle grazed the mountain's shoulder at a dead run, skimming into
the open air. Molly held her breath as the eagle's shadow streaked
down the slope.

We reached the crest of the ridge and found patches of blue snow
beneath the pines. Half-buried boulders protruded from a brown bed
of needles. Molly visited the overlooks. I lay on my back on a boulder,
pleasantly footsore and weary, watching purple-feathered clouds sail
through the canopy.

When an ant crawled over my hand, I woke from one of those brief
deep naps that last either a few minutes or a few hours.

Three vultures were circling low, grazing the pinetops. The birds
dipped and tilted in rigid flight, wings fixed. Their swift and outsize
shadows flitted from trunk to trunk with the stealth of mantises.

Darkness fell while I wasn't looking. Molly was nowhere in sight. I
called to her, but the sound of my own voice carried too far, startled
me, and disturbed the shadows. No answer came, and I did not dare
speak out again.

I recalled the woman in the cave, whom I had nearly come to disbe-
lieve in, and the remembrance touched the back of my neck. I had the
urge to turn and run the entire way down, shouting for Molly all the
way, but I was afraid to move or to speak. As I stood there, rooted to the
spot, I saw, far across the desert and low above the horizon, flights of
geese like so many broken necklaces drifting down the rivers of air. As
scarves of disintegrating silk they appeared, unweaving and weaving
on their long descent into the sun. I had a dim notion that Molly had
wandered that way, so I dropped a stone in my pocket and set off down
the far side of the ridge, onto the plain.

Miles on, under a cracked layer of cloud, I entered a shallow valley littered with half-dead campfires. Flakes of ash drifted low above the ground. In the middle of that valley stood a large yucca, its green leaves bristling like a brace of swords. The tall stalk burned, and each seed-pod burned, too, in dozens of discrete little flames, like a ritual cande-labrum. The yucca, enclosed in a dome of light, brightened in the gathering dark.

The earth trembled.

I turned to see several horsemen riding down at a lope. The lead horsemen passed without a glance, but a troop peeled off and, with leisurely laughter, circled the place where I stood. Bearded and skele-tal pikemen in motheaten cotton armor vests, wearing rusty helmets— morions, so called, in the Castilian style, crested and riveted and plumed.

With shouts, one of the troopers drove me toward the pack train, where the reins of a colt were placed into my hands. I began to walk, leading the colt as I was commanded.

Mules formed the van of the little convoy, their swaybacks draped with saddlebags brimming with turquoise and abalone shells. Across the animals' necks, like mock garlands, lay braces of headless turkeys tied together at the feet.

A file of human captives, roped at the neck, followed behind, shuf-fling barefoot in iron hobbles, their arms bound behind at the elbows.

That night, I fetched wood for the soldiers' fires, and water in leather buckets from a trickling spring, as I was told to do. I pulled thorns and needles from the warhorses' legs until nightfall, when I was permitted to lay down among the sheep and the mules. The captives lay along the ground like cordwood, hardly alive in their wounds and chains. They spoke in whispers and wept into one another's shoulders. I dared not do a thing to help them, but did only as I was told, and wanted only to outstare the nightmare.

The sky lapsed into light and we walked; lapsed into dark and we stopped. After a spell that was the mockery of time, we reached the prairies, where wind-plaited oceans of grass lapped against islands of pink sandstone.

Within the green seas of the prairies were the brown seas of the bison herds. Away in a far corner of that land were many hundreds of red-and-white-striped tipis. The soldiers gazed, exchanging observations in tones of wonder.

In the morning, a band of Indians approached on foot, led by a man with a red horn fastened to his forehead, and a shoe buckle hanging by a leather thong around his neck. The two parties traded captives—the Spaniards' old ones for the Indians' young ones—and parted ways in mutual and angry suspicion. A soldier led a girl by the arm to the pack train and set her on the colt's back.

We traveled till evening, retracing our route, and at day's end I performed my duties for the soldiers. At the pack train bivouac, I bathed the colt's legs with water. The girl fed him tufts of grass.

Midway along the next day's march, the girl halted the colt and climbed down to kneel in the path. With thumb and finger, she pinched a bit of black dust from the ground, rolled it between her fingers, and tasted it. She glanced toward the plodding soldiers, who dozed in their saddles in the noon sun, unmindful of the trail of dust they trod.

I observed in that moment how this black dust formed a straight line leading west, all the way to the horizon—how it marked the very path the soldiers, all unwittingly, were now following.

The desert at noon is tricky, when trees and stones retract their pointing shadows. It's a dangerous time to forget oneself, as the dozing soldiers had. Their horses, equally oblivious, followed their weary heads down the pale black road.

The bull roar clouted the air: flights of arrows heralded the ambush, and the Indians were among them before the arquebusiers could prime their weapons, or the troopers could couch their pikes. As the attackers commenced to batter the Spaniards with clubs, the girl ran away. I ran after her.

III

WHAT'S AILING YOU, BOY? MOLLY PRESSED HER HAND TO MY forehead. You been twitchin in your sleep like a puppy.

I'm okay, Molly. I have these weird dreams!

Sit down and tell me, Ray Moon. My dear old granny used to say that dreams were glimpses of the life to come, Molly said as she dropped two hot dogs in the pot.

I opened a can of chicken noodle soup, and said, I hope not, Molly. I told her every whit.

Aw, that's simple, Ray Moon. See, the girl, that's your future wife. And the bison'll be how many kids you'll have.

What about the man with the horn on his head? I asked. What about all the dying starving people?

Molly turned the issue in her mind, a touch somberly, as she stirred. That's your in-laws, she said.

Oh, Ray Moon. What do we do about money while we wait for the food to grow?

I don't know how I thought of it so quickly. It must have been in my mind, waiting for the weight of a single word to break the tension and spill it.

You can draw pictures of animals, I said, and sell them in town.

But I just draw birds, she said. Nobody needs another picture of a dang bird.

I think people would buy them, Molly, I said. There are stores in town that sell things like that. That place that sells the carpets and the Japanese helmets. They sell pictures, too. I saw em. And you're a good sketcher.

Sketcher, she said, and spooned up the soup with all the distraction she could muster. Horses are real tricky, but a pinyon jay I could manage. In a cactus. With mountains in the background. Good idea, Ray Moon! I'm gonna start tomorrow!

After lunch, while I followed Squeaky to its favorite precipitous cliff, Molly sat on the stoop with her knees drawn up and filled the air about her with thoughts and plans. When a police cruiser came thundering up the track, fishtailing through the sand and gravel, Molly called to me to go inside and bring a book to the back room and stay there.

I heard the two of them, Molly and the sheriff, enter the sleeper together. Molly's footsteps tracked lightly through the man's careless buckle and tramp. He resumed the orbit he'd commenced on his last visit, several weeks before, and his revolution around the room was attended by minor collisions, derisions, and the sour questionings of cheap booze.

I sat with the open book in my lap. As with every untimely thing, remembrance of his visits will always be attended by a very precise location and time. It's no secret that a conjunction exists between the body and the onset of trouble. But it's strange that the memory would take such pains to bind one's exact posture—whether standing or sitting or lying down—with a given event. Not only one's posture, but the unremarkable details of the hour: the grain of rice on the floor or the dusty cup on a wooden shelf will assume an awful significance, in the moment you realize that trouble has arrived and you have lost control.

I heard Molly pose a question, and I heard the man complain, and this was followed by that familiar laughter—the mirthless laughter he preserved, deep in his spleen, for such occasions.

The book I looked through during that hour was a picture book we'd recently acquired from Reginald Willie's truck. In one picture, boys play a game in which they attempt to throw a spear through a rolling hoop. In another picture, an old man stands amid his seated companions and reads out the scars on his skin like an illuminated manuscript.

The gasping quiet was broken by two curses followed by a crash and concluded with a boring lecture. Then I heard Molly speak.

I thought. But you said. About the money. I thought you said you—

I what? the man said shortly.

You told me you'd—

I told you what? I told you *what?*

The door slammed. The cruiser rattled off.

⸺

After the sheriff left, I came out from the room and found Molly slumped in a chair, holding a damp rag to her temple. With her eyes closed and her head tipped back from the pain, it seemed she was listening to a tiny voice relating very precise instructions on a matter of crushing importance.

This time, I did not hide away. This time, I took her hand, though I had no plan. After a moment, she opened her eyes and looked at me as though I were a stranger with a petty complaint.

Let's go outside, Molly, I said, and tugged. To my surprise, she rose from the chair and followed. I brushed the bottle-crate stoop with my sleeve and gestured her to sit, and she did.

There is this thing about people that I've learned. Sometimes they will begin to act, having no idea how the action is meant to unfold. But once underway, the purpose begins to resolve into focus, and oftentimes—surprisingly often, in fact—the action is proven to be sensible.

And so, with increasing confidence that my instincts were sound and that my efforts would bring her back round, I brought Squeaky from its pen and set it in her hands. The chick peeped and fretted in the cage of fingers, an ill-fed miscreant pilloried between her thumbs.

Molly leaned forward and laid her head on her arms and cried, while the chick, distressed and trapped in her extended hands, peeped in anguish, a meager offering to an old blind sky.

Time is not an indulgent creature, but neither is it a spiteful one. In time, Molly's welts subsided.

Her resilience fit a pattern. In the wake of the man's visitations, she retreated into a period of intense and private negotiations, during which I knew not to disturb her, and from which she emerged more or less willing to face the light again.

At the time, I imagined those negotiations as convocations that transpired in some smoky backroom of her mind, where she met with a delegation of livid spirits bringing not consolations but demands—a clutch of duplicitous gangsters, banging the table with fists, clamoring for endless concessions. Being phantoms, however malevolent, they were impotent in themselves, and eventually, after tormenting her for a time, they would accept her terms and suffer her to live.

She would emerge from those shakedowns—hungry, older—and speak a word to me. Let's take a walk, Ray Moon, she would say. Or, Let's look at a book together.

So it was on this occasion. Two days after the sheriff's departure, she came outside to the place where I sat with Squeaky, rested a hand on my shoulder, and said, Let's do school.

That's what she said: Let's do school.

From somewhere she'd gotten a hold of a deck of cards with illustrations on the backs. On each card, a word in Spanish appeared beneath its image.

We sat facing one another on the ground beneath the juniper. Molly fanned and burred the deck, then held up a card to me with her finger covering the word.

Guess, she said. It's a Spanish word.

I looked at the picture on the card, a befeathered Indian holding a spear.

I don't know Spanish, Molly, I said.

I don't neither, she said shortly, but this one's real easy. Now guess.

Indians, I said.

She looked secretly at the word and said, No, be specific. Name a tribe.

Comanche.

She looked at the card again like the word might change on her.

No, but good guess, she said. We read about these ones in the book. They used to shoot up the cavalry and hide in them woods along the river.

Apache.

She checked the card again. That's good, Ray Moon! El Apache. Look, it's the same word in Spanish, she said, and held the card out for me to see. El Apache!

There followed cards for rainbow and turtle—arco iris, tortuga— and the translations of those words were self-evident, because they betrayed a trace of their English equivalents: arch, tortoise. Absent such clues, we sought to discover tricks to remember the words by. For instance, the two els in "silla" resembled chair legs. That was my idea.

Doing school was fun.

⚬

Molly gathered up the cards and returned them to the shelf with our books. Then we packed some water and bread and the Boyda Book and embarked on what Molly called our Wildlife Lesson.

Before setting off, we stopped by the garden, as we always did, to see if there was any news. From one of the low mounds where Molly buried the corn seed, we were greeted by the tiny, apple-green blade of a seedling.

Molly set the satchel aside and stepped over the rabbit wire and knelt gently above the new life, laughing at the way it raised itself up—all proud as a pennant. I knelt beside her as she bespoke the first leaf.

Welcome, little corn plant, she said. Are you thirsty?

It was no surprise that the leaf spoke back.

I handed Molly our water bottle, and she let fall several drops about the stem.

What do we do now, Molly?

Nothing, boy. Let it grow. Watch for weeds. Give it a drink now and then. In a week or two, we can plant some beans around it. Then squash after that. They're called the three sisters, Ray Moon, corn and beans and squash. They help each other grow up good together. We follow the almanac, which follows the Hopis. If we keep our eyes and ears open, we might learn something.

She couldn't resist reaching a finger out to lightly brush the leaf, just once.

I found it impossible to believe that such a delicate thing had the slightest chance of living long enough to see the sun go down.

Ah, Ray Moon! Aint it wonderful? You and me helped this thing into the world, she said, But the work's only just begun. This is the world it's got to live in, and it isn't an easy place, so we gotta help it. You understand, boy?

I understand, Molly. I'll get horse poo and water for it every day.

Good boy, she said and climbed to her feet. Now let's leave this thing to its struggles.

We set off to the river for our lesson.

Many kinds of birds lived in the cane rushes along the bank. Molly flipped back and forth in the Boyda Book, but the little gray birds all looked the same, varying by slight degrees according to season and sex, so we gladly let them pass with their identities undisclosed. Moving with light steps through their realms, we brought letters of introduction in the form of quiet curiosity.

One small canyon was home to a clan of bluebirds, rare strange flowers on bobbing twigs. Molly begged their pardon and moved on.

The cane whispered, patient and biding, as though it had waited for years for a servant girl to slip through its stalks with a basket.

Molly spotted a bronze-and-red bird with a curved and ripping beak. She located the page that bore its likeness.

American kestrel, she said. We found one!

She wrote the bird's name in the back of the Boyda Book. She asked me for the date, but I didn't know.

Do you know what day it is?

I didn't know that either.

So she wrote the following: *American kestrel. breezy and sunny day but cold. Molly and Ray Moon. before lunch by the bluebird canyon.*

Molly, seated in a juniper's shadow, cross-checked her observations. By and by she closed her eyes, and the stub pencil slipped from her fingers.

A solitary cloud rose above the skyline. I recognized it as one of the ever-returning clouds I'd read about. The way it lingered there, bringing little besides a touch of color to the land and, it may be, an artless wish to look awhile on the windswept life it had left behind—a life I could not see from my seat beneath the tree.

While Molly dozed, I wandered off in the direction of that cloud. Eventually I came across a set of small footprints, and these I followed until I arrived at a burnt town.

In the courtyard of the mission stood a pecan tree, and from its branch a tonsured and bearded man in a brown robe was hanging by the neck, at the end of a braided rope. His bare feet dangled a palm's width from the ground, and his toes, it seemed, had traced invisible circles in the dust for days. In the hanged man's shadow stood a girl— the same I had seen on the way to the grasslands. She glanced indifferently at me, then resumed her study of the dead.

Turning away, I found strands of oakum lying about: a leather bottle, too, and a broken chain link, and a makeshift smithy where men, I suspected, had repaired their tack and blades. Beside the anvil was a fire in a circle of stones, where a little breeze stirred a flame from the ashes. An odor lingered about the place. Two vultures turned beneath the clouds.

A voice—fearful, demanding—called out behind me. Two men stood barefoot in the dust, hand in hand. Dried blood streaked down from their ears and eyes. I stood very still and did not answer, and they listened with grave mistrust to the wind, turning their faces to the smoke and the silence. The man called out once more, and I dared not breathe. Satisfied there was no one about, they proceeded to guide one another to the hedges behind the mission, there to seek by smell and touch the berries hidden in the thorns.

I followed the thread of a thin song to a doorless, unlit room and found a child, also blinded, singing a low song as he pulverized acorns with a pestle.

Inside the mission church, I encountered the girl again. Beneath the altar, she had found a bowl of cedar berries and three mice-gnawed cobs. The roof of the place had burned and caved, and the first flurries of the year whisked about like cattail seeds. Evening arrived in the company of late autumn cold. I gathered sticks of charred wood, the girl gathered tinder; she drilled the tinder in the old manner, and we lay down with the small fire between us. To my relief, she neither spoke nor looked at me.

At some bleak hour, I woke freezing and stirred the fire and prayed for the spell to break, for I feared this dream whose cold I'd begun to feel. A frenzy of bells cracked the dark like thunder, and the girl sat up and listened. The stars bore down through the splintered rafters. Shaken awake by the bells no doubt, the stars had come down to attend the tumult. When the tolling subsided, I heard someone speak from the shadows, and the girl answered in the language of that land.

A woman, dressed in a scarlet shawl, sat on a scorched bench and turned black yarn on a wooden winder. She spoke in a high, light voice to the girl, and they conversed across the dark. The girl glanced at me once, by way of an answer to some question, and in that glance I detected a severe impatience.

"I like young people," the woman said. "It's always trouble and tears, aint it? But there's no kindness fierce as theirs is, that's a truth. Did the bells waken you, children? Don't be frightened of them. The spirits of the bells are good souls. You and them are the only spirits in this whole country, anyhow."

The girl chided, again in her language, and the woman clicked her tongue.

"He's a nowadays child," the woman said. "You gotta take him along, girl, though he aint no help, I know."

"Grandmother," said the girl as she fed a stick to the flames, and now I kenned her words. "Is this the world where I have to live?"

"You know it is, child," she said, winding yarn.

"Will you help me find my home?"

"You know I will."

"But why do I gotta take this one along?"

"Don't speak harshly, girl. Anyhow, he's harmless."

The woman raised her work to eye level for closer inspection. The black yarn ball was transfixed on the winder like an apple on a fish spear. She resumed winding.

I kept my head down during that talk, feeling put upon and shamed, and rightly so, for I was lost in that place, and could not shake myself free of the dream, though I wished hard for it. When I looked up, the bench was empty, the woman gone.

Snowflakes like ash swirled in the darkness there. The girl lay in her cloak and slept. I lay down, too, in the certainty that I would wake up at home.

▲

But I didn't.

At first light, we scavenged among the charred ruins of the town and found a loaf inside a smashed oven. An old horse browsed behind a shed, too old for the girl's taking, so she unhobbled it. She set off westward on foot, with me following, toward the terraced mesas.

Barring the way north was a mountain range where drifting blue clouds left silver tracks of snow in their wakes.

The great gray goose of winter perched atop the highest peak. When it flapped and bugled, its wings drove ferocious winds across the uplands, and its song became a pounding squall.

All day the girl made her way across the desert, hardly resting, and in my weariness I trailed farther and farther behind. Then I began to sense, from her quickening pace, that she had entered familiar ground. When we came within sight of the cliff town, with its dwellings carved from the living stone, she paused, listening to the strange cries that carried in shreds to our ears.

She crouched behind a stone. The town was under assault.

Helmeted soldiers, partly concealed by a rising veil of smoke, occupied the overhanging ledge. The soldiers had rigged baskets to ropes and ropes to pulleys; now they lowered themselves to be level with the dwellings' mouths. While crossbowmen covered the operation, others attempted to heap brush at the entrances; by this stratagem they sought to smoke out the defenders.

At times the people inside managed to shove out the burning brush, creating fiery cascades. But the soldiers were persistent; they fed the piles and added pitch-dipped flambeaux to the fires. Those inhabitants who showed themselves, whether to extinguish the flames or sling stones, were fired upon.

Up and down the cliff face went the baskets filled with men—up and down went the smoking shouting baskets that resembled lamps burning dirty oil. Up and down the baskets went, like the broken shuttle of a loom, like a throng of infernal feasting spiders.

Once, twice, a man or woman crashed through the burning heaps and plunged to the rocks below.

The girl wept.

It was then we saw them: children and old people, women with infants, perhaps ten in all, clambering up the steep path toward our watching place. They passed on without a word, and we followed.

Evening found us among the boulders, crouched against the cold. Venus, with Jupiter in close attendance, brightened as the shadows rose. The streaming clouds blazed at last light, dragons sinking to their nightly beds.

No wood, no dung for a fire, no spark or food, no blankets. Snow fell and coated the ground, followed by winds that whipped up devils. Flushed from the earth, the snow gusts raced and whirled, apparitions incandescent with ice.

The girl died first.

A woman, wrapped in a scarlet shawl, mixed a bit of spit and dust and drew three lateral stripes across a child's brow. She sang, bowed over the child in her lap, and I knew the voice to be that of the yarn-winding woman from the ruined mission.

The cold bit but no longer burned, and I lay down with my hands folded between my knees.

Wake up, Ray Moon, Molly said, wake up now. You done slept through school.

IV

THE EARLY SPANISH EXPLORERS WHO CAME FROM MEXICO, I've read, had a saying about the life they found here: *ocho meses de invierno, cuatro meses de infierno.* Eight months of winter, four months of hell. Later I learned that this joke originated in La Mancha, in old Spain, which reveals a bit about the knight and his doleful countenance. But that's another story.

One afternoon, Molly and me lay side by side on our backs on the floor and listened as the wind picked at the sleeper's cracks. She said the wind made her nervous, but she had trouble explaining the matter. At last she said, It's like when someone hands you a plate of dinner and the noodles are touching the beans.

I could understand that.

The wind is tough on cattle and horses and carries an assortment of ailments for people. For these reasons the wind's arrival is for many an unwelcome event.

The wind holds an ambivalent charge, a sort of narcotic thrum between the eyes, a distress signal from a stricken ship that refuses to sink.

When the wind began to thunder out of a flawless sky, gusting to forty or fifty, I liked to walk outside. Molly never understood that. I wandered about, squint-eyed in the whipping cold, out in open ground, and felt the wind clout my ears as it snapped like canvas in a gale. Such a wind scatters thoughts, goads the gloom away, disorders (in a salutary way) the usual ways of seeing things. If only for a while.

Once, in a book we got from Reginald Willie's truck, I read a Navajo story in which these words were written: *The wind sustains life. When the winds fail, life will perish.* I recall those words every windy day of my life. When I see a leafy tree tossing its burly arms in a breeze—how it rejoices in a windy spring evening—I know that the words are true.

God brings forth the winds out of his treasuries, sang King David in one of his psalms. It's a pretty picture. Whenever I read that line, I imagine a lonely old man retrieving his dearest ribbons from a battered and bedizened sea chest.

Those ribbons, they surely remind Him of somebody.

—

The winds stayed a few days, then the sunny calm returned. In the morning, Molly went outside and filled two metal dog bowls with water and set them to warm on the stove, then sat at the card table and brushed her hair. She leaned over her knees and looked sidelong at the ratty carpet with a hazy calm in her eyes as she brushed. She assumed a faraway demeanor that suited the place she went to, wherever it was. For a time, while she brushed, her troubles dispersed, and her peace lent peace to the day.

Once the water in the bowls had warmed, she took one outside to the tree, where two small mirrors were fastened with roofing nails to the trunk. One mirror was fixed head-high to a child, and one was head-high to a woman: that is to say, one for each of us. There was a scuffed vinyl floor mat from some forgotten vehicle at the foot of the tree, which we stood on as we washed up. This was intended to limit the sand we tracked inside, but it was just a formality, for the red earth never failed to find its way everywhere.

When Molly returned from her toiletry, I carried the second bowl out and I found a note, a scrap of paper pinned with a thorn to the trunk, between Molly's mirror and mine. The note read, *I will learn about nature.* I don't know if Molly left it for herself or for me. She never mentioned it, and I didn't ask. I washed my face and hands and wiped my bowl clean with a dish towel and sat at the table with her. She told me of a terrible dream she'd had the night preceding, how she threw many cats out of a high window, one after the other, and didn't mislike doing it.

The wind probably gave me that idea, she said. Where else, she asked, would a thing like that come from?

We had just sat down at the broken fountain with a lunch of apples and tamales when P.D. pulled up in front of us on his bicycle.

Hi, P.D., Molly said, and offered him a pickle.

He glanced up and down the street.

Please understand that what I'm about to say must be kept confidential.

Okay, Molly said, and took a bite.

Today, he said, I must bicycle to Albuquerque to supervise the establishment of a new revolutionary cell. I'll return in two days' time. There will be a meeting of the Santa Juana Disciples on Saturday afternoon at two. I'm inviting you to join us.

Okay! That sounds wonderful!

Very good, he said. The meeting will take place in the back of Chang's Rattlesnake Museum. Head north on Indian 19 for one mile. On the left. Bring the boy. When you get there, you'll meet Chang the owner. He'll be seated at the front desk. You'll give him this watchword and he'll direct you to the meeting room. The watchword is: Coronado. Now repeat after me. Coronado.

Cordinado.

Close enough. So long, P.D. said, and he straddled his bike and was gone.

On Saturday, Molly and me hitched a ride to the turnoff for Indian 19. In the cab of a flatbed truck, the footwells were ankle-deep in dried brown lettuce leaves, and Molly thanked the farmer for his kindness.

Chang's Rattlesnake Museum was a low-slung adobe place with rotted vigas protruding like a battery of rusted and misaligned cannon from the deck of a half-sunk ship. A car and a pickup, a motorcycle and three bicycles were parked nose-first to the door like cattle at a trough.

Inside, a man with a belly and a Mongol moustache, seated behind a battle-scarred desk, harangued a lanky Amish teen. The kid wore a wide-brim straw hat with a sun-faded red band that had turned purple with the sweat of summers. On the teen's shoulder perched a redtail hawk that menaced the room with its gaze. The hawk cocked its head and froze us at fifteen paces.

You can't keep it here forever, the moustachioed man said to the kid. What I'm telling you is, is just bring some goddamn food for it, that's all I'm saying. I don't know what these fucking things eat, kid. I'm not gonna crawl around after a goddamn mouse for it. Look at the teeth on the sonofabitch. I bet it wouldn't be happy with no birdseed, kid. Am I right or wrong?

The teen smiled. Okay, Al.

Okay! That's the only word the kid knows! Okay! Jesus. Bring the bird in the back there. You better not be lying about that broken wing, man. If that sonofabitch starts flying around the room, its gonna run into my Slugger. Hit-and-run right through that window right there, see? This is a goddamn rattlesnake museum not a convalescent home for fucked-up birds.

Okay, Al.

Okay he says! Christ.

It was a rattlesnake museum. At least, that's what the sign said. But there were no rattlesnakes I could see. Molly approached a bird on a perch. CHIHUAHUAN RAVEN, stated the cardboard sign printed in green watercolor. Big as a chicken, with purple streaks in its tail, the raven emitted a low growl that was exponentially larger than itself.

The place flashed with birdcalls—parakeet and cockatiel—as with tin angels and pinwheels.

A rainbow-colored statue of the Holy Mother attended a parrot whose foot was fastened by a leather jess to a slender perch. The parrot shuffled fussily, seeming to betray some discomfort with the paradoxical nature of its predicament.

A middle-aged couple in white hats and white shorts guided a boy my own age into the museum. I watched him closely, which entailed no risk, for he was oblivious to human beings as he rushed here and there in heedless curiosity.

The boy pinched his nose with thumb and forefinger and reported back to his mom and dad.

I non't thee any rattlethnakes, he said.

The man behind the desk (it was plain by now that he was the eponymous Chang) observed the boy with mounting irritation, and at last dropped the newspaper and called across the room.

If it stinks to you, he said, then beat it. Does it stink in here, kid? Then hit the road.

The boy's parents guided him out.

Through the flyblown window, I watched the boy walk to the family camper, looking about him at the desert like he was lost in it. I wondered if that camper had a kitchen and a flush toilet in it. I'd heard talk of such marvels, but it was beyond belief.

Molly peered at a pair of house finches in a cage. She sang to them in a quiet voice—the birds listening with birdly distraction—until she noticed me waiting at her side.

Ray, she whispered, what was the password?

Coronado.

Okay, she said, I'm going to go and say the word to that man. I think that's Chang. He seems mean, though.

Chang's boots were kicked up on a desk strewn with gerbil bedding and birdseed. His head and shoulders were hidden by an opened edition of the *Santa Juana Sun News*. His fingers, clamped to the paper's margins, were stained with engine oil.

On the front page of the paper was a picture of a cow lying dead on the hard ground. I noticed, too, and with no little disconcertment, that it was June 23, 1968, for it said so at the top of the page. There was nothing about the date itself that startled me. It may have been 2068 for all I knew. What surprised me was that somebody out there in the world deemed it needful to number the days.

Molly stood before the man and said hello.

A moment passed before a corner of the paper fell. Chang looked at her and said, Buenas, lady. You want something?

Um, Cordandado?

¿Qué?

Corondado.

The paper collapsed in his lap, and he squinted in pain and said, What language you speaking, lady? Pick one and speak slowly.

Cor— Cora—

Coronado, I said.

Chang looked suspiciously from me to Molly and said, Are you people fucking with me?

Molly bent at the waist and whispered to him. Is there a man named P.D. here? We're supposed—

Oh, Jesus Christ. You mean Larry? You one a them? You look smarter than that, lady.

He cracked the paper at us and disappeared once more behind the photo of the dead cow.

Back there, he said. Look for the room full of silly sonsabitches who aint got any money.

᠁

The room spangled with song like a jungle dawn. The sweet smells of birdcrap, wood shavings, and seed conspired to plant a memory of cockatiels that flourishes in my brain to this day. Light fell, sluggish with dust, obliquely through the deep-set windows. The walls were lined with birdcages, and inside the regular square of the room was a circle of chairs, all but three of which were occupied.

A woman greeted us with a solicitous scoot of her chair, and we took seats. When I sat beside her, she took the measure of my soul in a glance, saw the sheep and the goats pastured there, and passed no judgment. I know this, because she reached out and cleared a bit of grit from my brow with a brief pass of her thumb. That was the first time I met Ingrid.

The racket of birds blotted every fourth word and hyphenated the low talk as we waited on P.D. to speak. He sat on the forward edge of the wooden folding chair, a sun-faded backpack lying slumped against his ankle. His beard poised on his face like a lantern from a fist, and he turned its light on each of us in turn.

I've been to the mountain, he said. I saw flood and famine in the land, I saw corruption riding on a black horse. I saw the earth despoiled by thieves, and the people oppressed and exploited for so long they've begun to see their degraded state as proper and good. This is what it means to be debased.

Molly pressed my hand, transmitting a secret awareness that P.D.'s words were not ordinary and possibly important.

P.D. got to his feet, steadily giving ground before his own agitation, and commenced to pace a circle within our circle of chairs. His words echoed in my ears for days afterward, and worked themselves into my memory as I recited them, again and again, back to myself. I don't claim to transcribe the letter of his talk with perfection, but what follows does chime with the spirit.

I saw the trees turn their backs on us, he said, and withhold their fruit. I saw the fields wither. The springs retreated into their caves and came not forth again, and the desert spread, spawning awful winds. The cattle, even, refused to be possessed by men anymore, and they fled back to the wilderness. And I saw the people call upon God, but he turned his back on them. Terrors and prodigies, great storms and droughts and star showers, all of these attended our abandonment.

His gait was stitched with a slight limp, and he strode his circle like a misbalanced roulette ball.

I saw the devil stalking the land, he said. And I saw the dead chop-

ping wood on the mountaintops. I saw a whole people defiled, in fet-
ters. Their spirit was corrupted by contact with a depraved power that
slaughters the innocent out of boredom, gorges itself to repletion on
the sweat of the poor, then sits back and counts its money. The world
steals, the world lies, and keeps the people in confusion so they can be
more easily . . . more easily . . .

And here he paused in his track, ransacking his mind for the right
word, a word slack and gross enough to contain the enormity of the
vileness that it signified. When he found it, the sour fire of the word
caused him to grimace, and he said: *managed.*

☙

Let's move on to survival skills, P.D. announced. The number one
problem to solve, he said, is hydration. Let's say we're all on the run
from the law. We're hiding out in the desert, or in the mountains. Or
let's say the feds have poisoned the water supply. What do we do for
water? What do we do?

With a covert glance through the doorway toward the counter, he
extracted a mason jar half-filled with hazy liquid from the backpack at
his feet.

In a pinch, he said, you can drink your own urine—

Molly nudged me, unnecessarily.

Now listen! P.D. said. You can't comprehend what I'm saying here
unless you've been in this situation. Let me tell you a story. I was south
of Laramie, riding to another town, on the way to visit a new revolutionary council. . .

His eyes closed on the memory, and his throat caught as if he'd
swallowed a bug.

I was nearly dead, he said, of thirst and exposure. I was nearly dead
from exhaustion.

He drew himself to the edge of the chair, as though someone had
grabbed him by the collar. He set the jar between his feet and bent his
head in a posture of frank submission to the fates that had brought
him on that day to that road south of Laramie, and in his mind he was

alone once again in the mountains and wind, far from shelter and warmth—a place from which, I suspected, he seemed to have never entirely returned. He extracted a brown phial from his tube sock.

And so I peed in my cup, he said, and I dropped two drops of iodine into it—like so.

He twisted off the jelly jar lid, added two drops to the pee with an eyedropper, then drained the jar in three gulps.

When Chang appeared in the doorway, P.D. set the jar out of sight, on the floor at his feet. Chang opened his mouth to speak, but something about P.D.'s demeanor checked him.

What's going on in here? Chang demanded.

Oh, it's all right, Mister Chang, said an elderly man. Larry's drinkin him some pee.

You better not be drinking pee in here, Larry. Look, one a you people's car is blocking the storage door and I gotta get some shit out.

Okay okay, P.D. said, painfully agitated, doubled in the chair, waving his hand blindly. Now go! Quickly!

Chang said, You better not be ordering me around, Larry, or I'll bust up this pee party faster than you can spit.

It's not a pee party!

Better not be, Chang said, and walked out.

P.D. returned the jar to the pack and said, Let's take this up at the next meeting. Now as a last order of business, I want to announce that I wish, *for the last time*, to no longer be referred to as Larry. Larry is the slave name by which the authorities keep track of me. So, from this moment I want to be referred to as P.D. How many times do I have to tell you people!

What's P.D. stand for? asked the elderly gentleman.

P.D. Prairie Dog. A rodent of the animal kingdom. Tunnel-digger. Root-eater. Survivor. One last thing, friends. I want everyone here to have a new name by the next meeting. A street name.

But I like my name, Larry, said the lady with cerulean eye shadow. P.D. I mean.

For reasons of security, and in order to maintain the integrity of this revolutionary council, I have to insist.

Molly squeezed my knee. I could see by her expression that she was conjuring aliases.

＊

Molly acquired a pair of binoculars—I'm unsure how—an outsize pair faded at the grips and fastened to a cracked leather strap. The instrument bore evidence of having spent many hours in a salt wind— scanning, I imagined, Atlantic horizons for Nazi subs.

During our walks, Molly took the bird guide and a satchel of apples and saltines; she let me carry the binoculars and charged me with its maintenance and care. I learned to tune the diopter and the wheel quickly to transfix a cactus wren on a cholla at forty yards, in the same way old folks might synch the tuning knobs on a shortwave to find that elusive Saturday night polka program out of Amarillo—which is to say, with a light touch.

As we set off, I looped the leather strap around my neck and experienced that rare and holy feeling called *a purpose in life.* The form of the instrument elicited that feeling, for there are very few perfect forms devised by human hands—the book, the bicycle, the violin are some—and binoculars are among them.

Picture someone shouldering a hoe or a shovel out to a bean patch at dawn: the tool informs her walk, the way she holds her head, the song she sings as she sets off to her labors. With the tool on her shoulder, she knows precisely what she is about, and has staked out a legitimate place in this universe, which is a damned uncommon achievement. It's a mysterious power a good tool confers.

We glimpsed a gray fox loping through the shadow of a rock overhang. The fox cast a single glance back at us as she crested the low ridge, paused at the skyline for a look-about, and vanished over the blind side.

Molly told me not to think about birds, and one would show itself.

But the mind is contrary. Like a rock in a glass room, it's bound to take flight.

As we clambered up through a canyon we were surprised by one of the ad hoc little traveling bands they call mixed flocks: sparrows, slate-blue juncos, and a bird we'd never seen. I can picture it clearly: green-feathered with a tattered red bib and a red cap like a tassel-less fez.

Molly consulted the guide.

Cassin's finch, she said, and looked from the book to the bird.

Cassin, she said. Who the heck is Cassin?

He must be the person who first seen it, Molly.

Is he sure of that? What a lot a nerve, y'ask me, she declared. Be off, bird. I un-name you.

The bird flew away.

You can't un-name it, Molly, I said.

Says who?

The Cassin's finch was the first name I entered in the bird list, but it didn't remain there long. Cassin's presumption rankled Molly, and she sought to revoke the proprietary license of the ornithologists, whoever they were. She ordered me to erase the name and insert a new one. The Cassin's finch became the Devil's Nightcap, for the fact of its red headgear, and so it was entered, with a stub pencil, on a blank back page of the Boyda Book.

Molly applied her own conventions to the art of naming, and she solicited my advice often. Soon, other birds were emancipated of their timeworn patronymics, and joined the list newly christened. Steller's jays became Bustle-birds, by dint of their fidgetiness. A Clark's nut-cracker, a rare pretty bird that lives high in the pines, shed its Anglo pedigree and became a Pine Moody, because the black-and-white pattern of its flight suggested to Molly something mercurial.

The birds were mighty indifferent to all this, of course, but it was a happy labor to free them from their categorical cages. It felt like God's work, in fact, which must involve a tearing down, a breaking apart, a clearing of the ground. Slipping tethers, loosing hobbles, leaving gates unlatched: that's God's work. Destruction comprises the better part of creation. Breaker bars and tire irons are the tools of His business.

On the days we wandered the hillsides, the birds showed little fear of us, and I imagined they derived a certain amusement from the silly things we said about them. It was understood that Molly and me were the morning's most purposeless creatures. We must have struck them as insane.

On the days we encountered few birds, and those far off, our spirits flagged. Their absence made us question our choices. They sensed, I suspected, ugly thoughts from far off and fled them. When the absence of wildlife became remarkable, it was then I studied my conscience. To this day, when I take a walk, I try to leave my little vanities at the tree line. Birds, like dogs and kids, can smell pretension like a cheap cologne.

Older now, I sit at the window with the Boyda Book, far from that place and that day. There's a discolored track along the fore edge that our thumbs made. There is sand grit between the pages still, and graphite stains inside the back cover where I'd listed the wildlife we'd seen.

Western bluebird
Scrub jay
Kangaroo rat
Thrasher
Western tanager
Horned toad
Kingbird
Gray fox
Tree swallow
Cactus wren
Yellow-headed blackbird

Nighthawk

Swallowtail

There is another list along the margin of an index page; this is Molly's bird nomenclature. There was no standard procedure, no Linnaean systemizing, no inspiration beside the color of a wing or the particular activity the bird in question was engaged in on the nameless morning when some strange woman in an olive field jacket and flip-flops wandered within its range.

Charity-bird, the second list began.

Twig-chatty. Blue rumor-bird.

Some names seemed to have derived from the bird's voice. Queeny. Home Come Home. Day-bells.

Others seemed behavior-based. Ribbon-thief. Pine-stitch. The boomerang bird.

Others wore their natures with their names. The lonely bird. The evening bird. The moon-brite.

⏤

I still carry the guide with me to the city park. A few years ago, along the walking path beside the lake, I witnessed a mobbing. That afternoon, the park was abandoned to gray mist, and I walked alone in common mourning with the bare, black earth. In other words, a typical Upper Midwest February day.

As I walked, a clamor erupted in a dead tree. The hawk, with long slate-blue shoulders, perched on the wet branch while, arrayed above and around it like funereal bunting, a few dozen crows preened and kraaked. The hawk tried twice to lift off but each time the crows mobbed it back to its branch, where it resumed its perch. I was convinced that, one way or another, the hawk would contrive to escape its tormenters.

The hawk's disdain for both my pity and the crow's hostility was a rebellion against the unremitting drear of the season. There was something lordly in its poise. It did not cry out or panic but sat scanning a meadow coated in mist and patchy snow.

Molly would have liked to have seen that mobbing. She would have clapped and shouted beneath that tree until the crows got aggravated and gave up. She would've liberated that hawk, unlike me.

Despair is an element in which all things live and move, an element so prevalent we might wander through days and years without remarking on it, unmindful as to how it sustains us and—it may be—nourishes us.

But it is not only that. The hawk's red tail touched the somber afternoon like a fingerprint, evidence or intimation of a power—near and unseen—a gathering of many waters in the sky. Some days, I feel, all that is needed is the weight of a syllable to break the surface tension, and there will be an end to things.

Night falls on a city, and the lights stretch away beneath the window, curving west by north along the shore. There are stars above the lake, and dull lights adorning distant freighters, and an old spirit moving over the face of the deep.

V

A GUST OF WIND, AND I LOOKED BACK. SLEET FELL WITH THE hiss of dead leaves skimming pond ice.

Deep winter. Horizons rolled away to the stone walls of compassing mountains whose slopes were marbled with blue snow. Cold locked the land. Out of whirling snow a people came, men and women, old people and children. In ragbound feet, bareheaded and barehanded they walked, decked in parti-colored cloaks or pine-green horse blankets. One woman wore a soldier's blue coat.

Foot soldiers flanked the column, rifles a-rest in the crooks of the arms. Bearded troopers rode along, mounted on black and branded chargers. Short carbines, ready to hand, protruded stock-first from saddle holsters. Now and then, the troopers raised whips and cursed.

A trooper, wearing badges of crossed rifles on his collars, pulled up in front of me. He handed down a snare drum and gestured to the strap, which I draped over one shoulder. He thrust a blue cap at me, and I put it on. He handed down a drumstick, muttered an order, and I turned and walked in the direction the people walked. I banged the drum as I went, one strike every two steps. That was my duty, and I did it well enough.

During that long walk, some fell out of the way. They lay on the ground and refused the hands that were offered. I passed a woman, seated beside the road. In attendance beside the woman stood a girl, and she was dressed in boots embroidered with dyed needles. Her hair was cut straight across her brow, and she wore a blue, short-tailed cavalry jacket fastened with a single gold button. I paused near them and dug a cob from my pocket. The woman shut her eyes. The girl looked at my hand and looked away.

At that moment a man halted above us. He was mounted on a tall horse whose hooves kicked stones and dust on the woman. He shouted and raised his arm over them and I dropped the drum and ran away.

Ray Moon, what's the matter? Molly said, pressing a hand to my forehead. I felt the warm weight of it and opened my eyes.

You don't seem well, she said. And you been pantin and twitchin like a puppy again. Are you dreamin of rabbits, boy?

It's the dreams again, I said.

Molly set a bowl of soup and two slices of white bread on the table. I sat and picked up the spoon. Frost fringed the window, and the pane was mottled with ice—but when I looked again I saw the usual sunlit desert beyond the sill and a black fly searching for a way out. In gratitude for an undeserved reprieve, I dipped the bread in the soup.

Molly, seated across from me, drew coyotes. In one picture, the coyote was curled about a litter of pups in tall grass. In another, the coyote loped across the page, past a flowering barrel cactus, and its eyes found the sketcher's eyes. Molly traced the coyote's jawline with one eye riveted on the pencil tip, like a dentist drilling a tooth.

Doves lit on the sleeper's roof, and in the stillness we heard their lonely calls. When they gathered near the roof vent, their voices filled the room.

Winnow May, Molly said. That's what I'm going to name my horse when I get a horse. Winnow May!

Where you going to get a horse, Molly? I asked.

She looked past me through the window.

I don't know, she said.

An hour after sunset, the sheriff's cruiser thundered up the lane. This time, I went into the back room without being asked. The man made his routine patrol of the place, his revolutions attended by minor curses and crashes and small mean gusts of laughter. They drank together, for I could hear the knock of a bottle on the table, and I heard her call him an SOB and other things.

I paged through my Indian book. I read closely, for by now the story had reached the days of the conquistadors, who had traveled past this very place, just as Fargo had told me.

In the crude old drawings executed by friars and untutored soldiers, I saw the very mountains that stood beyond our window, colored in red and brown, in shades of tobacco and copper and penny—just as they appeared today.

One picture I lingered over. In the scene, the people have constructed a makeshift gibbet of boards and planks, and they've hanged a priest, a Franciscan in sparrow-colored robe, sandals, and tonsure. The artist has captured not just the man's death, but his defeat as well, for the long slope of the shoulders betokened not just a broken neck, but a crushed spirit. The priest, head bowed and eyes pinned to his own dirty feet, seems suspended in a breathless shrug that expresses, all at once, the essential anguish of this world. It was as if the moon had been tied like an anchor stone to the priest's feet, and the weight of Jupiter draped across his shoulders. It was as if, on that day, the Indians had tried and sentenced and hung the universe entire. And perhaps, that day, the universe had deserved it.

As I examined the image of the man, all the boundaries that separated us vanished, and I found myself, a stranger, among the women and children, holding an armload of wood in my arms to place beneath the dead man's feet. For it was not enough to snap his neck. He had to be burnt.

The sheriff's visit ended with the usual groans and gripes and, himself replete, he made shift to be gone.

By this time, his third visit, I could envision, without seeing him, his precise movements, and even his expressions from moment to moment. I had yet to see the man's face, but I knew precisely what he looked like. As he paused with the door latch in his hand, I could see his expression as he turned to Molly.

You got nothin to be jealix of, he said. You my redhaired only girl.

In the morning I found Molly seated at the window, staring down miles of nothing. I made small noises to jostle her reveries, but she didn't stir.

Molly?

Go feed Squeaky, she said shortly.

Her grief overshadowed my chores. I mashed up some corn kernels and set them in the dish inside the little cage. The chick was beginning to fledge.

Squeaky, I said, I don't even know if you're a boy or a girl.

In fact, I didn't know much at all about Squeaky. I didn't know, for instance, if I was feeding it properly.

Squeaky, I said, What are you gonna be when you get big?

Squeaky peeped and pecked and cocked its head, waiting for even one question worthy of response. I crawled around and found a few sand fleas, squashed them between my fingers, put them in the dish; I added a little water and fresh sand and a few long grasses.

When I glanced at the sleeper, I saw Molly seated in the window, framed as though in a portrait. The light of her face was dulled by the dirty film on the glass. As she sat there, in a beaten slouch, her lips parted once; she spoke a single word to herself, one I could not hear.

I went inside and gathered Molly's animal sketches from where they'd been carelessly placed, and I said to her, Let's make frames for these pictures, Molly, and sell them in the town.

But she neither heard nor spoke.

I made picture frames out of scrap paper and rolled the works into a scroll, and the next morning we set off for town. Halfway there, without a word, she turned off the asphalt and into the desert.

She paused to pick up a stone here, a stone there. I followed at a distance, so as not to distract her, and did not know what purpose she had in mind as she made her methodical way up a dry stream bed, stone leading on to stone like a trail of breadcrumbs.

At the head of the gulch, she emerged into light, her figure spliced against the blue sky. Like a seed-caster in search of new acres, she scanned the horizon, overlooking land I could not see.

When we arrived in town, I followed Molly from corner to corner, looking for a place to display her wares.

Too much sun here, she said at one intersection.

Too windy, she said at the next.

Someone peed here, she stated at yet another corner. She sniffed the air like a fox and kept on.

At the next corner, she squinted at her shoes and held her breath. No, she said. I can't think good here.

Finally, we sat down at the corner of Main and Silver, in front of the Daytime Hamburger diner. She reasoned that families would come in and out. But at first all who passed were truckers and farmers who paid no mind to nobody.

One rancher seemed inclined to complain but refrained for lack of sufficient grounds. He looked about, disappointed in finding no officers of the law at hand. He entered the diner, finally, having resolved to forget this outrageous world, where vagabonds sold trash with impunity in public.

Molly set out the pictures three by three, each weighted with one of the small stones she had gleaned on the way. Now I understood their purposes, for the color of each stone harmonized with the colors of its assigned postcard. We seated ourselves before the drawings, now anchored and neatly arrayed, and awaited paying customers.

A mother and child passed. Unblinking, Molly followed the pair as they receded, the woman's hand gripping his tightly, the boy tripping along. Molly stared after them, and I wondered if she was pained to be discovered there on the sidewalk—and by a woman her own age, no less. No, it was not embarrassment. She recalled herself from a distant place and found me waiting here.

Ah, Ray Moon, she said, ruffling my hair. Did you see that woman's shoes? I bet she could click her heels and fly away to Kansas.

Others passed, and a few slowed to catch Molly's eye. Some lingered, a touch bewildered, above the pencil sketches, so lovingly arranged, of a Tortoise and a Coyote, a Roadrunner and a Devil's Nightcap. A nun in head-to-toe white habit praised the pictures. A plain cotton wimple framed a face that appeared younger than Molly's, and she carried a scuffed black case containing, I assume, a flute or a clarinet. She hitched the strap behind one shoulder and leaned over for a look.

Where did you learn to draw? she asked.

Learn? Molly said. I never learned.

The woman slipped a change purse from the folds of her skirt. How much does that one cost? she asked, pointing to the roadrunner.

How much?

One dollar, I said. Right, Molly?

One dollar! Oh, yes! Thank you, Sister!

Molly set the bill in the empty square where the picture had been, then weighted it with the same pink stone. The rancher came out and stood over us. Some hot food had done him good, for he gave me a wink as he hitched his belt.

Sold one, huh? he said to Molly.

He squatted and picked up the jackrabbit picture and said, My granddaughter's nuts about rabbits. How much you want for it?

One dollar!

One dollar? Lady, you're sellin yourself short. Take two.

No one else bought anything that morning, and that was fine. Molly was beside herself as we gathered up the unsold merchandise. She skipped and sang and hugged me twice, and we bought strawberry ices at a stand and had enough left over for a can of Treet and a sack of tortillas, a jar of peanut butter and a Zigzag bar that we ate on the hoof.

As we crossed the square, we encountered P.D. Molly told him how she'd sold three postcards.

Three of em! she said. And look at all this good stuff me and Ray Moon got!

He peered into the sack and praised the food.

She tore a tortilla in two and handed half to P.D. and half to me.

Put me down for a drawing, too, Molly, he said.

But you haven't even seen em, P.D.!

If your heart is filled with light, he said, then the things you create will be filled with light, too.

Molly flushed a bit at the neck, which was a thing I never saw, and it was nice to see.

P.D. saw it as well, and his eyes fell to his hands. A thought occurred to him, then, and his face brightened as at a piece of good news.

Hitler painted postcards, too, he said.

Really? Molly said. Were they good?

Were they good? Well, I guess I don't know the answer to that. You know, Molly, that was a stupid thing I said. Hitler! Gee, I'm sorry.

Why are you sorry, P.D.? It's important to know Hitler painted postcards. I think people oughtta know that.

I think you're right, Molly, he said. Maybe people oughtta know that.

For a moment, the words lived in the sunlit space between them. I think P.D. suffered in the presence of charity, even a small charity, having too long deprived himself of such things. But he lingered on the spot and warmed himself briefly in the light of Molly's kindness.

He told us to be at Chang's Rattlesnake Museum in an hour for a meeting on survival skills, and with an awkward decency that caused him discomfort, he took her hand, pressed it, and walked off, cursing himself for god-knows-what reason.

⚊

During the long walk back to the mesa, a man stopped and offered us a ride. But there were kids and dogs in the back seat, so I begged off.

After extracting a promise to go straight home and to stay off the highway, Molly let me go alone. I set off into the desert.

I didn't go straight to the sleeper but wandered till the sun sailed behind a cloud. I turned back, after an hour's walk, to find the mesa had dropped from sight. The sky had acquired a silvered depth—shadow-clouded—that reflected the dark land like an antique mirror.

The land stretched away to emptiness at every horizon. Fixing the sun to my back, I kept a straight course. A long walk brought me to a garden of stones—stones tall as spires—that had been planted in that empty plain. Human figures were painted on those tall narrow stones, and I mistook them for living beings—all of them depicted in poses of arrested violence. To my mind, as I passed by them, they seemed to question me about my origin, my destination, my name. I passed through with only those ferocious demons for company, my every step dogged by their enormous tormented eyes, until darkness obscured their faces.

A great fire burned in the distance, and many animals fled past me in the dark, shapes that I could not name. I slept on the black stone, curled beneath a greasewood shrub. In the morning, I found the mountains cloaked in ice.

The inverse image of a golden city appeared above the rising sun, a brace of transposed towers blazing with lights like a candelabrum pending from the apex of heaven. The barefoot blessed, playing pipes and timbrels, walked in file toward that celestial town. Their long hair hung loose about their shoulders, they wore robes scrubbed to snowy brightness by the desert wind and sun, and to my dejection they neither looked upon nor answered me.

Molly woke me.

Them dreams, she said, are making you pale, boy.

⚊

Molly took to sitting for hours beside the window, deep in the desolate precincts of the hurt she endured. And yet, she never forgot to prepare coffee for us in the evening.

While I read, and Molly waited for the water to boil, she hummed songs, and the songs she hummed recalled, with their mild mournful air, something of green hills and heather and rain. I did not ask her what melodies they were, or where she'd learned them. I am sorry for that.

Sometimes, listening to her voice, I read without understanding, or forgot the page altogether. Then I'd look up to find the window had filled with darkness.

At that time, I did not know what loneliness was. For a child, it's just a state of things, as predictable as the noon hour. A common condition, like wakefulness or sleep. An affliction not to be questioned, but simply carried to term, and then, perhaps, for a brief time, put aside.

But the loneliness of childhood has this quality: it is visionary. Childhood confers a measure of neutrality that allows the child to wander freely between worlds. The inattention and perpetual distraction of guardians constitutes a safe-conduct pass through their many arbitrary jurisdictions.

Powerless, the child possesses power indeed.

Unacknowledged by authority, the child often finds herself above suspicion, and she might, if she chooses, take what she wants and get away with it. But finding so little of value among the things reckoned by society as precious and therefore forbidden, she will generally leave things as she found them. In this way, she justifies the trust of her keepers, but not for the reasons they tell themselves.

Innocent of hierarchies (by virtue of inhabiting the lowest level) she is indifferent to all scales of worth. She wanders without judgment, then, with plenty of time to record the passage of a ghost on a shadow box of her own creation, the operation of which will always remain a mystery to good citizens who, in any case, could not be bothered to care what she's up to.

*

In the old story, the two orchard thieves are discovered in the theft of an apple and are called by the Creator to account. Half asleep they had dwelt in the days before time, but they were shaken to life in the wake of the theft and banished to a world of succession and of change, a world they could hardly abide.

Adam and Eve were thrust into the exile of this world. With them it was a wakeful trauma. With us, it's otherwise. We are born to it, and we grow very slowly into this strange indifferent life, and—by some unaccountable grace—some of us make a sort of home in it. In such meager ways does the universe indulge us.

During the time I knew her, Molly was young. Naturally I didn't realize this. Looking back, I believe she was experiencing the first intimations of exile, the knowledge of which comes at last to everyone. Her loneliness became, with each day, less an object to dwell on, and more of a mode of existence, one that had been prepared for her from the foundation of the world, a fact as ineluctable as the night or the law.

I don't know if she imagined any means to escape it. Her loneliness squatted on the desert and gazed on her. And now, with the advent of the sheriff, the loneliness was joined by its old companion, fear. Like two hungry cats, the loneliness and the fear maintained their hungry watches, out in the middle distance beyond the window.

Convoluted allegories, airy abstractions! Let's be truthful: loneliness is a wicked strain of insanity, and, in the final analysis, I was not very good company.

Molly, I said. Is that man who comes here, is he your boyfriend?

Seated at the window, she didn't blink.

No, Ray Moon, she said. He's just a man.

🔹

A motorbike climbed the track, sidewinding through the sand, steered by a woman wearing aviator goggles and loose long hair. I recognized her from the secret meeting at Chang's. She pulled up in front of the sleeper, dropped a bare dusty foot to the ground, killed the motor, pushed her goggles up, and shouted Hello! Anybody home?

Hi, Ingrid! Molly said as she held the door open. How did you know we lived here?

Didn't you say you lived on the mesa? There's only three trailers up here, Molly. The secret's out!

Molly pulled a chair up, put a pan of water on the burner, and opened the can of coffee while fending off Ingrid's protestations.

Hi there, baby, Ingrid said to me. What are you two doing today?

I'm looking at a book, I said to her, and Molly's looking out the window.

It was not my habit to effuse to a semi-stranger, but Ingrid had a way of eliciting the truth from every creature in her vicinity. She wore the expression of one amused by things that had never entered my mind but would soon enough. I sensed that there was nothing under the sun that could remain concealed from her for long. If such a presence sounds oppressive, I suppose it is, for there are many who dislike sharing space with a person like Ingrid. To me, though, her knowingness was merely liberating, for I was spared the exertions of pretense. That was not difficult—my mean habits, needless to say, had not yet ripened into age.

Molly didn't mind it either. She had little fear of being known.

You two need to get out sometimes, Ingrid said. You're starting to look like each other.

It was good to see Molly laugh. Two of her animal sketches lay on the table. Ingrid picked up one.

It's beautiful, she said.

She sat, took a small brown bottle from her bra, and poured a dash of cough syrup into her coffee. She held the bottle over Molly's cup, with an inquiring nick of the chin, and Molly assented with a blink.

It's Irish coffee, Molly. You seem Irish, so it's okay.

Come here, baby, Ingrid said, and pulled me to her knee and caught the corner of my eye.

You're a big boy, she said. Soon the girls'll be sitting on your knee, is that right?

Embarrassed, I climbed off and opened my book. It's funny the way women talk around small boys. They commence with the poking and jibing, the little mortifications committed with a grin. I don't blame them. They probably figure they might get their licks in while they can. They know well that the boy will become a man and that the man will return it sevenfold.

Molly made a coffee for me, but I wouldn't have any, out of stubbornness. I regret it still. It's stubbornness that makes a life miserable. Acts of stubbornness accumulate over the span of a life, like plaque on the brain, and make the ending wretcheder than it need be.

Your hair is beautiful today, Molly, Ingrid said.

I looked at the page without seeing it, listening the while, marveling inwardly at Molly and Ingrid's easy talk, like ones who had known each other for years. Ingrid's was a careless kindness. She carried kindness the way the cloud carried Helen.

I soon forgot my wounded little pride and made a sandwich for Ingrid.

Sweet boy. Molly, you're doing a good job raising this boy up in the right way. There aint enough men who know how to be kind. My old man used to beat me for a witch, she said. He broke his back cutting timber and now he slobbers all alone in a chair like a goddamn vegetable. Don't be scared, though, I don't know nothing about no evil spells. Anyway, witchery aint inmissible in court no more, you know.

If I were a witch, Ingrid continued, I'd a brought my pouch of potions. But all I got is a bottle of Broncleer and two cans of Olympia.

The two women shared a can of beer and chatted in a manner that sent me about my own business.

I lay on my stomach in the corner and opened the book.

Now, a rain cloud, according to the book, resembles a stack of cannonballs, and a snow cloud is a stack of blocks, and a Spaniard is a man prone, eyes closed, with a spear planted in his chest, and a woman is the seed-planter who carries a brace of arrows on her back.

Come here Ray Moon, Molly said, and handed me a can. I took a drink.

I've been quiet toward him, she said to Ingrid, and they shared a wondering look at me—curious, amused, uncertain. They talked about me as if I weren't standing right in front of them.

Come here, little son of a somebody, Ingrid said, and she pulled me onto her knee again.

Will you turn me into a vegetable, Ingrid?

Worse than that! When I get done, she said, it'll be better for you if you'd never been born.

Molly choked on a swallow of beer.

Now put a shirt on, boy, Ingrid said. We're going to town. You two gotta help me today.

⁂

The motorbike slalomed down the track to the highway, with me seated between the two of them.

Ingrid called above the throttle and wind, Can you write good, Molly?

No, but Ray Moon can!

And that's how I became the amanuensis.

The county infirmary—hospicio, they called it—squatted on waste ground at the edge of town. From the rear of the building we entered an empty corridor lined with doors, each differently painted in bright colors, yellow and red and green. The doors were closed, all was still. Ingrid paused before the blue door, listened a moment, knocked gently, and turned the knob.

An old man was asleep on a cot in a room that was bare but for two wooden chairs, a crucifix bearing a hand-carved Christ with bloody knees, and a Sacred Heart posted high with two dried flowers tucked behind the frame. The sunshine passed through the gauzy curtain to fill the room with a light dry and clean as birds' eggs.

Ingrid handed me a notebook and a pencil, and I took a seat next to Molly. Beside the man was an IV drip stand and a metal tray bearing rolls of gauze. Ingrid lightly pressed two fingers to his temples.

He opened his eyes and scanned the ceiling for the Angelus hovering there, or the common tern of omen. Finding nothing on high but peeled paint, however, he settled back into his bones. He pressed Ingrid's hand to his heart and closed his eyes. Down the hall, a door closed, and the curtain in our room billowed once, lightly, in a breath of air. When Ingrid glanced at me, I opened the notebook to the first page and waited, pencil poised.

Hello, Erwin. How are you, man? You remember my name?

You're Ingrid.

That's right. Do you remember what we were talking about yesterday? Before you fell asleep?

I do. We talked of my daughter, he said. She died of meningitis, age about eleven.

You were telling me, Erwin, how she was such a darling. What else do you remember? Don't be hurried. Molly, will you get us a glass of water? Just ask Berta at the desk by the front door.

Erwin swallowed and smiled. Oh, she loved to swim, he said.

I wrote the words down, just like he said them: *O. She loved to swim.*

He spoke with precision, with a parched weariness that no water would relieve, and I did not miss a syllable.

She swam in the river every day, he said. One year was dry. The river dwindled away to nearly nothing. But she went anyway, every day, as it got smaller and smaller, dryin up till it was just a string of muddy pools. She always found a bit of water, though, even only a bit, just a little to dip her fingers in. Yes, even only the tips of her fingers, at the end.

He swallowed with effort. Ingrid smoothed his forehead. A breeze lay down, the curtain stilled.

I was helpless, he said. One morning the river was all gone. On that day, October the third, nineteen hundred and thirty-nine, the child was past comfort.

I wrote it all down. The workmanlike care of the old man's speech, I believed, was partly in consideration of the scribe, for although Erwin never did turn his face to me, I knew without doubt that my presence, and my task, were known to him.

Molly returned with a glass of water. She held Erwin's head in the cup of her hand as he raised himself in his feebleness to drink.

Refreshed, he lay back and breathed freely. His voice brought his hands and eyes to life, and he saw again the eleven-year-old girl, dead these thirty years, as plain as the flaked paint on the ceiling. Ingrid sat with her ear to him, her head bowed a little.

Will my child be my child still, he asked, when I meet her again?

Ingrid glanced over her shoulder at Molly and said, I don't know, Erwin. Maybe yes and no. The best part of her, she said, will remain true, even more than true, and the rest of it maybe won't matter too much. But that's just a guess, Erwin. Your guess is good as mine.

Tears brimmed in his eyes at this piece of news that might've been a lot worse, and he fell asleep in that moment.

Ingrid pulled the blanket over his shoulder. That's enough for today, old man, she said and turned to me. Well, my son? Did you get all that?

Truly, I didn't miss a syllable. If Erwin dropped a G from his -ing, then that's how I wrote it.

Molly asked, in a low voice, Who's gonna read these words, Ingrid?

We'll give them to a loved one, she said, if such a one can be found. If not, the words'll be buried with the body. The body has a way of forgetting. Wherever he's going, he might wish he had something to talk about. So I see to it that the words go along with them.

With her eyes on the sleeping man, Molly asked, What about bad memories?

I don't ask people to tell me happy stories. They usually don't. Sometimes they do. But you know, all our stories have somewhat of life and somewhat of death in them. They all have both. So it's not really got to do with good and bad.

We returned to the hospice several times to record stories. I don't know, looking back, whether Ingrid's was a paid position or if she was a registered volunteer or a licensed caregiver, as we might say these days. I never saw her sign a clipboard or punch a clock or present an identification card. She walked in and out of that place like she'd been commissioned—whether by herself or some proper authority was unclear to me, and doubtless of little concern to her.

Ingrid drove us home and joined us on a visit to the garden. The corn seedlings had grown three inches in as many days.

I shouldered the basket and set off for some horse pats while Ingrid and Molly, by studying the mounds and the wind and the sun's ecliptic, plotted for beans.

They planted the beans around the corn, within a mixed bed of manure and dry earth, and let me add a little water.

Ingrid said her grandmother used to plant in this way. She declared that the woman—who suffered neither careless hands nor tongues— would not, if she were here today, scorn our little garden. The good word made Molly glad.

After the second visit to the hospicio, as we were walking along the road back to town, we encountered the Great Migration of the Tumbleweeds.

Gales of pewter-colored dust veiled the distance that afternoon, and the mountains receded into shadows till only wavering guesses of ridgelines remained. The deserted plaza had been scoured of trash by a cold wind by the time we arrived there. A man with a white beard leaned against a light post at the long-distance bus stop, his hand resting on a pool cue as on a shepherd's crook. It was as though Steve McQueen had fallen asleep in a cave for seventeen years and returned to town to find the pool hall abandoned and the Greyhound running several months behind schedule. The man watched Molly, as we crossed the street, with a look of thirsty disappointment.

Grackles perched on a swaying powerline, levering their tails to keep balance.

The wind goaded wild streams of weeds and dust down every east-running street. We approached a corner and paused before stepping into the wind-stream, like two pilgrims at the edge of a snowmelt river. Just then, a tumbleweed—big as a medicine ball—went bounding head over heels down the pavement.

Man alive! said Molly. There goes grandma tumblewheel!

And right on grandma's heels came five little tumblers, bumping and leaping, pouncing along like a litter of wolf cubs, and crossed the intersection without looking. We waded into the street and saw, two blocks away, the main waves hurtling toward us. Along every alley and lane, the tumbleweeds passed through the town.

The dead thistles had spent the winter out in the desert, patiently withering, and when the clarion sounded, they severed the final fiber of their roots and began to move, singly and in pairs, then by clans and tribes, nudging one another into life and action. Most people only see the scouts and outriders of these migrations, but sometimes, if the proper wind follows the proper dry spell, thousands and tens of thousands will be on the move together.

Such a herd passed through Santa Juana that day. The first and fastest sprinted past, then the rest followed in a rough cascade, a wall-to-wall whispering stampede. From the edge of town to the foot of the mountains, the entire land was in a ferment, as though ten thousand jackrabbits had been flushed by a rumor.

We took seats on a rail line embankment, a few feet above the flood. The migration, after its initial novelty wore off, assumed the quality of something almost purposeful—as though all creation, suddenly sentient, was charging headlong to a summons.

In the midst of that migration, in swirling dust, the seasons changed, and I was alone.

We are walking, she and I. Stars wheel above a mountaintop.

"Where are we going, Yarnwinder, ma'am?"

"Back. Where else then?"

"How far is it?"

"Far!"

A light cracked dead ahead. An old man appeared at the crest of the ridge, and the man and the light were one and the same. With his back to us, he unfurled his wings, and his wings were the plaited layers of dawnlight—the coverts, the secondaries, the primaries so called.

The colors of the wings were the stark colors of an old devotion, when the gods or demons mixed egg white and stone dust to paint birds' wings in lapis, cinnabar, radium green. With the spreading of the old man's wings, the darkness began to seep like water into the sands.

By now we stood beneath his mountain. It was about the fourth hour, and the colors of the day were arranged in discrete and level layers—just as gravels, bearing the colors of their distinct ages, bed down along a river's bank. A pool of blue gathered at the apex of the sky, where the last three stars slowly drowned.

His business finished, the man sat slumped with his back turned to us. His crown—the color of lamp brass stained from ages of dirty oil—was tilted and tipped.

As we drew near, he did not stir at the old woman's cheery greeting.

"He must be angry at me," she said. "Or at you, boy."

She halted and leaned back and roared at the mountaintop, where the old man perched, as all around him the day brightened by degrees. "I'm small, but you listen to me!" she yelled.

"Who's there? Oh! Forgive me, sister. Did you call to me? This old body don't hear so good."

"Oh, that. Me neither. Old man, tell me! How do I get this one back to his home?"

"I'll show you," he said. He tipped a flask onto his fingertip, then flung a grain of sand high into the air. The grain hung there, suspended from nothing. Each of the grain's facets was a speculum in which was reflected the things that were and the things that will be.

In that grain, we saw a vast open pit. Mountains had tipped down its slopes in crumbling rockslides; rivers plunged from its lip and vanished into mists. Broken highways teetered over the pit's lip, dangling wrenched I-beams and raveled rebar.

The old woman spoke quietly now. "Did prairie dogs dig that hole, old man?"

"Keep walking," said the angel of the sun. "You keep walking and see for yourself whether prairie dogs dug that."

"That pit lies near to where I first set eyes on you, old man, all them years ago."

"Even so."

"It cannot be," she said to herself, riveted on the catastrophe revealed in the facet of the grain.

The grain fell back into the angel's hand, and he returned it to the flask.

She shook her gaze free and shouted, "I'm small, but you listen to me! Help me make this right. I know you know how to fix this mess."

"Not this time, sister," he said softly. By now he bore the full light of the day on his trembling shoulders. "I'm too old. You go and see what you can do."

She hurried on, and I followed. The wind rose and the sand blew and the day went dark.

⚓

The days warmed by touches. Molly and I filled a basin with dirty clothes and hiked down to the riverside. We stretched the cleaned clothes across boulders to dry, weighted these with stones so they didn't blow away, and wandered apart to find shallow pools to wash in.

A few trees grew along the stony bank, and the afternoon sun let fall its shadows on the water. In the shade of an overhanging tree, I lay back on a boulder to dry, electrified by the alternating currents of sun and breeze. I shut my eyes, and the violet world revolved beneath my eyelids.

I heard the coo-call of the nest song from an unseen dove, and I knew then that summer had arrived. A blue shadow crept up the copper-colored cliff face as the sun mounted. Dry leaves on a scrub oak, burnished to copper by fierce winters, rattled in a light breeze and scattered flickering light on the deeper pools near the water's edge. I fell asleep.

I woke to find Molly splashing through the shallow bankwater toward me. On her back was a small round boat, and she carried it as a turtle carries its shell. In shape, the boat was somewhat like the fairy goblet of an acorn cup. Light and round, the boat was a seamless hide stretched over a wicker frame, with a narrow seat board spanning its waist. The diameter roughly matched the height of myself. She set it in the shallows.

Molly, I said, what is that thing?

It's a boat, Ray Moon. Fargo told me people use these things in Asia to do their water-farming. He said the old saints floated across oceans on em, too. Look at this, Ray Moon: Fargo tarred it and tightened it up and gave it to me. I've kept it hidden in the reeds back along there. Nobody found it, neither—it was all covered up good.

What are you gonna do with it, Molly?

She faced downstream, shaded her eyes with a free hand. A leather satchel hung from her shoulder like a seed-bag.

I'm gonna see if it floats, Ray Moon, she said. Come along.

Molly led the boat into deeper water, and we climbed in. The thing floated indeed, and we sat on the board and laughed, for floating on water is a ridiculous thing to those unused to it. Molly used a long branch to punt us into the main stream. As we drifted down the river, Molly poled from boulders as one fends off bergs. I peered forward—a pale figurehead in a pair of white underwear—and called out *boulder! boulder!* like a half-drunk helmsman.

When we reached a stretch of still water, Molly settled with the paddle athwart her lap, satisfied at her own facility with the craft. She was one born to water, it seemed. There's an old story, from the Irish I think, that I read years later, about a man searching for home. When you reach land, he's told, you must burn the boat on the shore; walk inland, then, carrying the oar with you. Keep walking until you reach the place where the people ask you, *What is that thing in your hand?* Build a small fire there, for you've reached your destination.

They call this kinda boat a coracle, Molly said.

A what, Molly?

A coracle, she said.

She repeated the word, coracle, liking the savor of the word, glancing about as she said it—*coracle*—as if seeking a fair excuse to cast a spell with it.

The land looked otherwise from midstream. The hills and mountains showed other faces to the river—faces hidden from highway travelers—faces scarred with rockfall. The cliffs, I understood, would not conceal their fearsome age from the river, for it was the river itself that had aged them.

The sun stood high at the mountains' shoulders, the sky vaulted the rubble heaps of the hills, and the land turned in long shining bends, revealing solitudes as we drifted.

Blue and yellow birds appeared low above the surface, hovered there, and dropped like stones to tap the water with their beaks, touching off concentric rings. The birds tapped, lifted off, resumed their hover-patterns, tapped again—sounding the day with jewelers' hammers.

When we sluiced between two great boulders, I gave a yelp, then we resumed our placid glide. On a hilltop overlooking the water was perched a great stone that, but for some sorcery, should long ago have tumbled down. Molly pointed to it, tapped her lips with her finger, and the stone suffered us to pass. When we neared a foaming pool that whirled in the lee of an immense boulder, we paddled clear with our hands, frightened and exultant.

The birds tapped, the tune infected the sky, the sky answered with silence. In this way, the water-loving birds arranged the peace of the day into song, while the river bore us along.

●

I don't know how far we traveled that afternoon. Two miles, maybe nine, maybe thirteen. We might have entered another state for all I know—long enough, at any rate, to satisfy Molly's curiosity on some point in question, which she did not share with me. At a shallow stretch of water, she planted the stick in the bed, pushed hard, and angled for the shore.

A canvas strap was fastened lengthwise to the seat board of the coracle, and a person could fit the strap around their chest and carry the boat quite easily in this manner—as I was saying, like a turtle her shell. So I strapped the boat on and followed Molly at a right angle from the riverbank, due west, knowing we'd come to the highway by and by. And so we did, after an hour's hike.

The man who gave us a lift did not inquire after the coracle, for it was a thing beyond his experience, and therefore beyond his ken; for this reason the coracle was, strange to say, not even visible to him. Having no word for it, he simply didn't see it. His willful inability to notice the thing was infectious, so much so I found myself looking back, again and again, to confirm its presence in the bed of the truck. There are a lot of things men refuse to notice, though they be under their very noses. Well, it's a common affliction.

We arrived at the sleeper that evening, having hitched and walked a long way. I had just stowed the boat around the back when the red lights of a cruiser broke the dark. The vehicle ground to a halt in front of the door and waited there, its light bar flashing. The candy-colored light played on the wall like some lurid, buck-fifty flick on a drive-in screen. Then the lights and motor cut off, the night closed in, and I waited for the man to climb out. But the door did not open, and the cruiser gathered the night to itself.

Molly spoke my name and pointed to the door. I entered and closed myself in the back room. Through the walls, from outside, came voices but not words, questions but not answers, and simple pleas from Molly that cut no ice with the man.

❧

During the days that followed, as the shadow of the juniper told the hours in its turning, Molly stayed in the sleeper. A few times, she took out a sheaf of wrinkled blue paper—her brother's letters—and read them through, page by page, front to back, first to last. The blue bruises yellowed as they faded.

I set a book on the table before her. On a strip of tanned hide, a

Cheyenne artist had chronicled the victory over Custer's troopers. Sprawled horses, arranged in rows and still saddled, were flecked with the rose florets of wounds. These were the dead cavalry horses. The dead soldiers were tallied in bloody handprints, and Molly counted them all. She was moved by the carnage, and whispered numbers as she drew a finger down the columns, like a Florentine banker perusing the Duke's catastrophic expenses.

Two hundred seventy, she said.

Those were the first words she spoke in six days.

That night, there came a knock at the door, and she listened without moving to the silence that followed. I peered from a corner of the curtain.

It's Fargo, Molly, I said.

She smoothed her hair with her hands, opened the door, and averted her face as she welcomed him inside. He wiped his boots on the patch of carpet and said, after a moment, Don't be ashamed, girl. What happened?

It's okay, Fargo.

That sheriff did this, isn't it?

It's okay.

You and the boy come on over to stay. Won't nobody bother you there. I can promise you that.

Thanks. But no, man. You're kind. Don't worry.

I wisht I'd a been a better neighbor to you. That animal.

Never mind it.

She invited him in for a coffee. As he waited, he regarded me with cool though kindly regard, just as he assessed every living creature.

When she placed the cup in his hands, he thanked her and said to me, You want to go for a ride, kid? Put some warm clothes on. I want to show you something. You too, Molly, if you like. I already packed a little food for us for the ride. It's somewhat of a ways from here.

I sat between them in the cab of Fargo's truck. We drove an hour on the highway, then turned onto a ranch road. No one talked, nor was talk welcome, for it was a moonless dark, the sort of dark that made voices strange, one's own most of all.

The motor's roar was underscored by the night air whistling through the vents, and the juddering ride splintered my thoughts. I slipped into and out of a doze, waking each time to find the headlights illuminating a tract of scrub that hardly changed. The Milky Way unfurled across the windshield in a wordless speech banner.

When the truck came to a stop, I woke to find myself face to face with a mountain. We climbed out and followed Fargo along a path that wended up and up among tumbled boulders, up toward the stars that had commenced to blanch with the coming day. As we reached the crest, the earth gave sudden way to dawn and wind, and we stood freely in the open, breathing hard.

At our feet, an immense white desert rolled away to lap at the base of another range of mountains, one situated at the eastern horizon, a range which mirrored, so to speak, the range on which we stood.

A violet band backlit the eastern range. Like woken dragons, the mountains stirred in their nests and bulked with light.

Molly handed me an apple. Its skin was cool as creekstone.

We took seats among the rocks. Far below, white winds commenced to stir the gypsum sands.

⸙

Imagine a city of marble, built long ago on a dry seabed, a city whose inhabitants were one day carried off by some mysterious cataclysm, the nature of which no longer matters. Imagine the city's slow return to the earth, over the course of millennia: the timeless decay, the infinitesimal thefts by wind and sun, the intricate care with which they dismantle the kingdoms of man. So loving, it seems, so solicitous, one almost suspects a hint of mockery, an insult administered with such courtesy it leaves the victim feeling flattered.

In the center of that city stood a temple, and inside the temple sat a stone goddess on a marble throne.

The temple was once painted in primary colors: the columns painted blue; the roof bright orange; and the incarcerated goddess wore sea-green eyes and golden hair.

But invaders smashed the goddess; disasters scattered her votaries.

Time passes. The temple roof collapses and the vivid colors fade until only a picket of naked columns remains. Periodically, over the ages, a raven lights on one of those fading roofless columns. The bird croaks for its mate, extends its swept-back wings, flaps once, twice; it leans into the wind and lifts off. And as it rises, it brushes away a mote of dust from the top of that column. In this manner—mote, by mote, by mote—the pride of men is demolished, and their proudest works consigned to oblivion.

The statues, grottoes, arcades of that city disintegrated into their constituent dust, until they lay heaped in the bone-colored dunes you see today—dunes whose clean crests are embellished with beetle tracks—or stitched with the paw prints of a lorn coyote. The white sands are all that remain.

The ravens still carom like billiard cues in the wind, seeking out the high buffetings, there to tumble and roll like children at the shore. Wings extended, they are happily overtaken in waves of wind, as they always have been: from the age of unrecorded calamities, down through the voiceless centuries, down to the days of the turquoise traders and the uranium miners, to this very morning's three unin-vited visitors—bright-eyed with watchfulness and lack of sleep—who are seated among the high rocks.

As we looked on, slender beams of sun streamed through the nocks of the eastern passes. Like golden oars, they lowered as the sun rose, until they came to rest on the desert surface.

I heard a voice say, This is where it all began.

A moment passed before I realized it was not me that spoke.

The soldiers dug trenches over there, Fargo said, about thirty miles that direction.

He gestured vaguely toward the north, where the darker basin land stretched away.

The soldiers were given goggles, he said, and told not to look right at it. Like an arc light—it might blind you. Then they set off that bomb and the winds came pounding at the soldiers' backs. The air stayed scorched for days. Burnt air. He could still smell it, years later, when he told me the story.

Who?

My father. My father told me how fire flew up into the sky. Some soldiers said it flew up like a giant bird. They all crouched in the trenches and looked at that bird. And that bird looked back at them. That bird never stopped looking at my father, till the day he died. Even then.

Molly looked over the desert. The hurt yellow moons under her eyes gleamed in the half-light. I see the bird, Fargo, she said.

That's good. Keep it in the corner of your eye. And don't let it see you.

We returned to the sleeper that night. Fargo left us at the door and continued to his home. Before she entered, Molly noticed tire tracks that veered behind the sleeper. She ran to the back and stood at the edge of a tract of ruined ground where the little plants had been. The mounds were crushed, the rabbit wire tangled and buried in places where a vehicle's tires had backed and filled over the little garden. Molly knelt and ran her fingers gently though the turned earth, feeling for seedlings. She lit a match and passed it slowly over the ground.

I crawled about the garden's edge for a long time, lighting match after match, probing here and there for a living leaf.

Molly spoke my name. I rose to my knees to find her standing with a pack on her shoulder. She did not look at the ground.

Come, she said, and turned.

I followed.

We climbed into the truck. Engine parts lay scattered on the floor-boards.

Now, that truck's transmission had been a source of anguish in the final months of my uncle's life. Several times he removed and tinkered with the thing, but he could never get the grind out of it. Fargo, over the previous weeks, had removed and retooled the gearbox. Perhaps he'd had an inkling that Molly would soon have need of the old truck. I was there to clean the parts and to hand him tools, so I knew that the job was not entirely finished. The shift knob was missing, and the shift stick protruded from a hole in the floor. The shifter, in fact, was not even attached. I told Molly the thing was drivable, for I'd watched Fargo work through the gears many times. I began to explain how she had to joggle the stick to engage it, but she could not listen to me in that moment. She clenched the wheel in her fists and tried, it seemed to me, to claw out of her own body. When the tension broke, she heaved for breath, and the sweat ran in coffee-colored drops down her arms.

At last, calm again, she wiped her face and said, Tell me again.

I did. I showed her how to fish for the proper links, blindly, with the shifter.

Molly turned the ignition, engaged the gear, and the truck shot forward. Soon we were beating down the highway in the dark.

A cruiser with red lights flashing overtook us, cut us off, and slowed. Both vehicles came to stop in the middle of the deserted highway. The truck's headlights lit up the cruiser, and we watched the driver put his hat on, climb out, and walk toward the driver door.

The sheriff knocked on the window and Molly cranked it down without looking at him. He shined his flashlight at her, then me.

Where you off to, Molly?

She didn't answer.

He turned the light on the shifter sticking up through a hole in the floor.

Looks like that Indian, he said, been playing with this junk. This machine is not roadworthy. I'll have to give you a ride home. I'll call my friend Bobby to send a wrecker.

It drives fine, Molly said, her teeth clenched, staring through the windshield. We got a right to drive it, too. Anywhere we want. So you move your car and let us go on.

I'm afraid not, Molly. Your headlights are out. You can't drive at night without headlights. That's a state law.

Finally she turned to face him. He stepped to the front of the truck, slipped the nightstick from his belt, and punched the butt-end through the glass of the left headlamp, shattering the bulb. He did the same to the right one, and the night darkened by magnitudes. Then he stepped around to her door.

Like I said. Headlights are out.

She flung the door open and jumped down, picked a handful of gravel from the shoulder and flung it at him. The pebbles rattled like buckshot against his cruiser, and he shielded his face with his hand as Molly hurled another handful, and another, and shouted at me to get the pack. I could not see her, but I could hear her steps as she headed into the desert. I followed until I caught sight of a figure, on her knees in the sand, clutching her stomach as she retched.

🔹

I heated a can of beans with two slices of spam, but Molly ate nothing. She sat beside the window and kept watch on the empty track that meandered down to the desert floor, and when she saw that I was finished with the meal, she shouldered the satchel without a word and walked out. Through the window, I saw her set off down the track with the coracle on her back, a pair of legs in yellow trousers porting a weathered brown shell of a boat, like a tortoise traveling from water to water. I followed at a distance.

We made the long walk to the river's edge and found it deserted but for a clan of noisy scrub jays. Molly unstrapped the boat and stood it end on, inspecting as she rotated it. She dropped the boat in the water, held it steady for me and, for the second time, we set off down-river.

We passed the familiar landmarks, and I recalled aloud the names we had bestowed during the first voyage.

The Shivering Cliffs, I said. The Balancing Stone. The Whirlpool.

We passed the utmost point of that voyage and kept on, wary and alert, sleep-deprived, shoeless as pilgrims, and kept our eyes skinned for cataracts.

The land darkened on both banks as we passed through the clinker fields that spilled down from the cinder cone. The badlands—malpaís—where a people once hid in lava tubes and where the Spaniards' horses could not follow. Molly punted for the shore. There we put our shoes on, anchored the coracle with a stone, and set off.

The few scattered junipers fell behind as we set off across the fissured rock.

There was no birdsong; no paths crossed that place. As we made our way, the hills neither drew nearer nor receded, and the wind blew the hot dry sunlight in our faces. After an hour's walk, we lost sight of the river. Molly glanced at the sky.

What time did we leave home, Ray Moon?

The question surprised me. I don't know, Molly, I said.

She stood atop a smooth stone with her ankles together, like a gull on a pier post.

It's about noon, she said, and it's July. That means the sun is south of us, high, and setting west.

She about-faced and named each horizon in turn.

North, south, east, west, she said. The river's that way. When it's time to go back to the boat, we'll walk away from our shadows. Then we'll come to the river.

Without another word she continued toward the dead volcano.

I don't know when Molly learned to read shadows, whether she got it from a book or puzzled the matter out in her head. While I was wool-gathering by the window or daydreaming beside Squeaky's pen, she'd been acquiring knowledges.

What appeared to be a grove of maypoles in the distance turned out to be a forest of dry trees. Limbless, leafless, shorn of bark, they seemed to have erupted fully grown from the black rock. The smooth trunks—sun-varnished and wind-lacquered, tapered like so many sharpened sticks planted hilt-first in the earth—stood spliced against the sky. They didn't bow and wave in the wind like living trees, but were as hard as the rock they grew from. Nor was the rock sterile, but was splashed with gold and green lichen that provided sustenance for whiptails.

A dream recalled itself and the place became known to me all of a sudden. I hop-stepped quickly across the stones until we came to the mouth of the familiar cave.

Molly! I said. This is the place I told you about, where I met the woman in the mask that day I got lost and had a dream.

The dirt around the entrance was scuffed, and the inside was swept smooth. Molly climbed down after me and we stood together on the sand floor. The small circle of stones contained cold ash and cinders.

Do you think they still come here?

I don't know, I said.

The living procession of chiseled images, ascending the wall in a helix, had vanished.

I'll bring my brother to this place, Molly said. When he comes home, I'll bring him here. It's a good place. No one will follow us. Here he'll get his spirits back. You did good to remember it, boy.

We rested for a time, because Molly was unwell. She lay on her side for an hour, holding her stomach. When she was able, we set off for the river, walking away from our shadows. Just as Molly had reckoned, we arrived directly at the coracle. I strapped the craft to my back, and we set off upstream on foot along the bank.

Midway along the return journey, we noticed a quick-moving wall of rain setting on from behind us.

Molly said, Watch that volcano, Ray Moon. If it disappears in that cloud, it's probably hail. In that case we'll have to hunker.

Sure enough, that volcano disappeared. In minutes the storm

overtook us there among the stones, and Molly and me crouched on our knees beneath the coracle. Molly kept us covered as hailstones drummed the upturned craft and the wind's gritty fingers tried to pry the thing from her grip. The pounding hail roared like the ocean and, curled up and dry, I fell asleep there.

The misty shadow of the pit cast a gray bow into the sky, and we walked toward it. A trembling bellow rose from the pit, intensifying as we approached. At the edge, the yarnwinder woman paused.

She picked up a short stick, fastened a scrap of red cloth to one end, and tossed it over. For a long moment, the stick plummeted through swirling mists, twisting in a crash pattern. I followed the scrap of red with my eyes until it was swallowed in a green cloud.

In shape, the pit was an inverted cone. Two roads, each cut into the wall of the pit, spiraled from the cone's tail to its lip; the roads ran clockwise and counterclockwise, like left and right-hand threaded screws—a double helix so-called, narrowing as it descended.

The roads led downward and upward. Being congruent—mirror images of one another, in fact—they intersected at a thousand points. Both roads bore endless convoys of front-end loaders and earthmovers. The roaring coughing machines paused with remarkable solicitude for one another at the crossings. With impeccable and timely deference—without signal or traffic cop—they preserved the right-of-way.

Halfway down the steep, road-scored walls of the pit, gray clouds floated like barrage balloons above the Dover coast, obscuring the nadir of the mine. The depths exhaled a steady draft of damp air laced with diesel smoke and bitter water and stone, bathing our faces with the sour breath of a dragon's cave.

From the depths, came people.

They climbed hand over hand, step by step, by a path dim as a goat track to my eyes, a path running at right angles to the muddy narrow roads. Men, women, old people, children emerged from the pit onto the flat earth. The level light of the setting sun, shining in their faces, drew tears from their eyes, and the old folks wiped the dirt and sweat from the children's brows.

Ingrid emerged with them, wearing a black knit cap on her bald head.

"Ingrid," I said, but she didn't hear me, or she didn't want to.

"Another dramatic escape, huh?" said the old woman.

"By the skin of my teeth, Yarnwinder," answered Ingrid, and walked on.

"What did she escape from, Yarnwinder?" I asked.

"From the monster, boy. Don't you know nothing?"

The people clambered, singly and in pairs, over the lip of the mine and onto the sunlit earth. They walked west, where the great armillary of the sun—five brass hoops nesting one within the other, spinning on five separate axes—had begun to sink. Throwing off volcanic sparks, the sun interred itself without a sound.

The sound of raindrops on the roof woke me.

Molly dragged the rain barrel beneath the sleeper's low corner, and we took seats beneath the juniper. After so many dry days, the air was heavy with the iron smell of earth. The stones gleamed against the dark ground. The rain fell with such a startling gentleness, I was worried lest an idle word would spook it. Molly felt the same, I think, for she sat very still and didn't speak. The rain lingered only a while, just long enough for a few drops to trickle through the branches and down my neck.

The raincloud turned its back on us, slipped over the mesa's edge, and set off across the open desert: a spectral giant in cloak and hood striding the good earth on two trick knees.

A grateful shadow kept the surface moisture alive for a few more moments, and I pressed both palms to the cold sand, and the fresh damp seeped like medicine into my knuckle bones.

That rain cloud's passage signaled the monsoon, which in this place amounts to little more than a few brief July showers. The margin of survival, measured in millimeters.

During monsoon days, the clouds resemble icebergs, pristine blue peaks atop immense thunderclouds. The thunderclouds, steeped in livid dust, drift at the horizon line—a chain of magic islands trailing torn roots of rain that never touch the ground.

A clan of quail lived in patch of creosote at the mesa's base. We never failed to rediscover them because they weren't very fast, they flushed easy, and they didn't fear the open ground between cover, which was alarming behavior for a plump little thing in a hungry place. Molly wondered if the quail lacked intelligence, then felt bad for slandering them, and finally decided they weren't thick-witted after all. The males looked downright worldly with plumes of feathers bobbing from their heads, like Mughal princes fussing busily among their gardens, oblivious to the troubles broiling just beyond the palace walls.

We came to recognize roadrunner tracks by the capital X of their prints, and when we set eyes on the birds themselves—which was rarely, for they were hunters not gambolers—we admired the blue and red feathers streaking their temples. That dash of color had a touch of the pagan about it and bespoke bloody rituals.

A few species of desert bird, we noted, wear a brief splash of color—roadrunners, flickers—and we debated the purposes of such extravagances. The roadrunner's war stripe, Molly decided, was an act of sedition. It marked him as chosen, or doomed, which may amount to the same thing. Flamboyant and unpremeditated the stripe was: the way a man might tuck a rose in his buttonhole on the way to an engagement where he was sure to meet enemies and ladies.

At the very dawn of time, it may be, all desert birds sported outrageous plumage, dramatic displays born of God's volcanic fancy, in the days when He was young.

In that moment, a pair of doves raced past.

Once upon a time, Molly said, the dove was bright orange, not gray like these days.

From her words I conjured an image of a pair of orange doves perched on a dead branch like two candle flames on a skeleton's fingertip. The image returns every time I hear a mourning dove, even to this day.

Molly changed the subject. Perhaps she was careful to ration these visions against the lean days to come—to not burn them all up at once, but to sustain herself with a morsel at a time, like a pocketful of bread crumbs. Two orange doves: that was quite enough for one day.

Our list of birds and bushes and animals, observed and described, crept down the margin of the back cover of the Boyda Book.

The book contained no information on stones, however, and Molly viewed this as an omission of singular absentmindedness. That a stone is not a life-form and should find no place in a biotic survey is an assumption that carried no weight with her. The error was mine as well, insofar as I shared in the book's wooden-headed prejudices. I was trapped in arbitrary categories and fixed ways of seeing—mired in received wisdoms of which I am both inheritor and servant, and for which Molly had little patience. Stones were possessed of beauty and purpose; by whose right should they be excluded from the book of life?

That evening, we returned to the sleeper to find Squeaky's cage smashed in the dust, and tire tracks doubled over the spot, and the bird, nearly fledged, lay crushed in its blood.

I wrapped the body in a red handkerchief and carried it down to the desert floor, down to the cemetery. There, I scratched a shallow grave beside the diminishing mound where my uncle lay.

I was not aware that Molly had followed me to that place, and her presence startled me when she knelt at my side. She dropped a few oatmeal flakes beside the bird, then I covered it with sand and stones.

In shame I realized that Squeaky's life had remained to the end a mystery to me.

I didn't even know whether its destiny led to rooster-hood or hen-hood, or something no man had ever dreamed of.

⬥

Molly placed a call at the telephone booth outside the post office. Whom she called, she didn't say; but I suspected, by the way she slouched against the wall and picked absently at the booth's chipped paint with a fingernail, that she was speaking with family. She listened with eyes closed, and after a few half-hearted queries, she hung up.

We walked to town to visit the food pantry, where the nice ladies gave Molly a cardboard box containing rice and cornflakes and cans of green beans, along with a paper sack of tomatoes and white and green onions.

As we entered the plaza, we saw P.D. declaiming beside the dead fountain. Foremost among the audience of eight or nine was a man wearing a Kaiser moustache and a soiled cowboy hat pulled low over the eyes, who nodded with indiscriminate satisfaction at every word.

P.D. menaced his auditors like a thunderhead.

A strategic blunder, he said, of monumental proportions! They started this war thinking their rear area was secure, but it isn't! Little did they perceive the threat looming right here. Now they'll have to wage a war on two fronts.

He took a step forward, lowered the pitch, and drew the words out of his gut, with painful precision, like the thread of a suture.

History suggests, he said, that such a war cannot be sustained. Ask Hitler. Ask Napoleon. Ask Rome!

Two women strolled arm-in-arm through the plaza, talking as they watched, glancing sidealong at him. Two men exited the diner and paused on the sidewalk to listen.

Just then the bells in the belfry of La Anunciación began to toll the noon service, and P.D. perked like a fox.

What! The church says, Look here, and the priest says, Look here, and the governor says, Look here! Here is peace, here is sustenance, here is security. Follow us! But these are all lies, because the son of man himself hath not where to lay his head. But if you believe the bells, Go, follow them. The church bells have tongues, people say, but the tongues lie. Our Christ was a homeless criminal, and he was executed for that reason, but their Christ is meek and mild, a helpless victim. The time is coming when every lie will be exposed, and every truth revealed. An army of free children is coming, and they're bringing new laws—

Molly put her arm around my shoulder, which was a thing she didn't often do. Her gesture caused me to look about for trouble. The sheriff stood in the shadow of the plaza's lone tree, one thumb hitched in his holster belt, smoking, maintaining a bored disregard for the speaker. Two ranchers who stood near him exchanged leers with the cop, who took the cue.

Where's this army at, Larry? the sheriff said. Say, Larry, where's this army of kids with guns?

A laugh trickled across the plaza.

P.D. seemed for a moment to stand a few ounces more heavily in his shoes. He rocked once in place like a tree and took the measure of his thoughts.

He said, I hear someone asking, Who's been walking in my vineyard, plucking grapes? I hear someone asking, Who's been fishing in my stream? I hear someone saying, Who has built a fire on my hilltop? I see someone coming, wrapped in the robes of his own justice, bringing tortures and prisons, prisons and laws and more laws. What do we say now? How should we answer that man?

Some of the few who remained looked back to read the sheriff's expression, but I don't know what they saw, for the man's face was obscured by overhanging leaves. I could see a leg of blue trouser with silver piping and a holster riding slack on one hip. The man who wore these things kept his arms crossed and didn't move.

P.D. said, I see someone coming. An evil man, one intoxicated with malice. And I see another, a daughter of righteousness, who will stand against him in the fullness of time. Many will accuse her for a troublemaker, they'll call her by evil names, they'll slander and abuse her. That's to be expected. Here is the truth.

His words lengthened as he lowered his voice. For only a moment, he had their attention; for just a moment, no one smiled or looked away.

Here is the truth, he said. It will go hardly for that evil man on that day. I don't know what God has in store for me, because I'm not a good man. But I do know what God has in store for the likes of him.

It was then that P.D. spotted Molly standing off, and his eyes brightened in recognition.

Molly waved and said, Wave to him, Ray Moon. I did.

P.D. said, My army's here, sheriff, in answer to your question. They're standing all around you. You have eyes but you can't see them. You've never wanted to see them, which will prove to be a grievous mistake. But I won't be the one to lead that army, I'm just telling you what's to come. When the chosen one arrives, I won't be worthy to polish the buckles of her shoes.

P.D.'s shoulders dropped, and he spoke with hopeless care. The one who will come after me, he said, will not tolerate the injustice and cruelty that you carry into the world.

With a pretense of laughter, the ranchers turned away, and the last of the crowd departed with them. The speaker had possessed only enough interest to delay them for a time. It cost them nothing, after all, to let a lunatic rave.

But the man with the black Kaiser moustache—arms crossed and head cocked—remained. He nodded, eyes closed, at the echoes of the speaker's goodly dream.

P.D. crossed the plaza to the place where we stood. He stopped before Molly, touched her elbow with his fingers. When he saw the yellow half-moons beneath her eyes, tears sprang into his own.

Molly, he said.

She blinked as though he'd called her a thief.

I could see, through the space between them, the big tree in the plaza. The sheriff had stepped out from beneath its shadow, and now he stood alone in the light of day. The heel of one hand rested casually on his holster belt, the other hand along the hem of his trousers. The breast of his boiled uniform gleamed with a recent ironing. The bill of his visor cast a dark ribbon across the bridge of his nose, and his face was turned a few degrees from our direction, so that I could not tell what he was looking at.

There is often nothing distinguishing about cruelty, a wise woman once noted, nothing remarkable in its voice or appearance. Now, if a cruel person were marked like Cain, or wore a beetling brow, or had the white scar of a lightning strike across the bridge of his nose, or had a sneering lip or a cold eye . . . but it's not so. Theirs are often the most forgettable of faces. The truth is, from that day on the plaza of Santa Juana de Arco, when we listened to P.D.'s speech, to this day, many years later, as I sit beside the window in my thirteenth-floor apartment, I have not been able to recall a single detail of the man's face.

P.D. took one of Molly's hands in both of his.

Molly, he said, the stars of insurrection are soon to rise. Now I have to visit the cities of the plain and inform the cells that the time has come to gird themselves for battle. When the war begins, things will happen quickly, and we won't have much time. But I hope that you . . . I hope we . . . that is to say, will you wait for me? There's something I want to ask you!

Of course, P.D., Molly said, a touch unsettled, but not unhappily so. She patted his hand, and he ran off.

At the post office, a letter from Molly's brother was waiting, and I walked ahead of her down the highway, so she could read without having to watch her feet.

Ray Moon, she said, folding the letter. Tommy'll be home in two months! We have to plan a party! It'll be so nice to have him home. You two will get along like gangbusters. You know, the more I think on it, you two are so much alike. Ah, it'll be good to have him home!

We arrived at the sleeper in high spirits, and she sang songs as we wiped the dust from the windows.

Tuesday's pantry supplies generally held out till Saturday. The difference was made up by the sale of painted postcards—and by Ingrid, who showed up on Sundays and Mondays with paper sacks of corn tamales and cans of beer. Fargo, too, left timely bags of potatoes and onions by the door, and he never failed to fill our water tank whenever he filled his own.

Also, a bit of cash remained from the forest firemen, but we used it to buy books from the book truck. It had been the unspoken condition attaching to the forest fire money: it was not to be spent on perishable things like food and shoes. But that rule was cast aside when things got tight.

Molly read to me in the evening as we sat on chairs facing the sunset. When she grew tired of reading, I read to her.

One evening I opened a collection we acquired from the book truck. I happened on a story about a woman who, in fleeing from her pursuer, prayed desperately to the earth for help. And the earth heard her prayers, and changed her into a laurel tree, impervious to human cruelty.

I enjoyed the story and told Molly so. I wished aloud we might live in a world of daily miraculous escapes. And with that I closed the book, set it aside, and picked up a second. I had entirely forgotten the matter when Molly spoke out in a sharp tone.

Raymond, she said, Don't read them books if you're gonna read lazy.

Her words confused and hurt. At the time, I didn't understand that, to her mind, the story did not conclude when the woman took root, and that things did not end because you reached the final page. There remains the necessity of telling and retelling one another our versions of the events we experienced together, that we might verify the sequence, recall forgotten incidents, check our understanding against our companions'. There remains the necessity of imagining what happens next and—if need be—of fashioning from our own hearts and minds the things to come.

Every single thing that happens survives for a time within the living memory of those who took part. But those people pass away, one by one, until the memory is the possession of a single soul, and only with their demise does the living memory expire. At that point, there follows a long diminishment, as the descendants, and those who knew the story secondhand, pass away in their turns, until there remains only a silent and solitary consultation of books—and this, too, by fewer and fewer people. The books, then, are handed on, or thrown out, or find their unlikely ways into the bed of a pickup with New Mexico plates and the word BOOKS stenciled on the tailgate, driven by a man named Reginald Willie. There, along with a few score other homeless stories, they end their days on a jouncing circuit from town to high desert town, trailer to lonely trailer, resigned to an unpromising search for someone to take them in, until the driver grows too tired or too poor to put gas in the tank. That's how the story ends.

But Molly did not believe it.

On the final page of certain books (it's not so common these days) you'll find the words THE END. But in older books, ones printed in old countries, instead of THE END, you find the word EXPLICIT, which means *to unravel*—a legacy of the days when stories were read from scrolls.

For Molly, I believe, books were intended to be unraveled—not opened and closed. This unraveling, she understood, was the business of the living. Delinquency in this task was an abrogation of what amounted to óur obligation to those who have passed before us.

Molly wouldn't have put things like that, but she was angry at the way I'd concluded a story that clearly wasn't finished. Therefore, the next evening, Molly told me to read again the story of the woman who was transformed into a tree—to read slowly, aloud, and from the beginning. To read with care, to let the story fall word by word into the good soil, and strike a root there.

And as I read the story again, she listened calmly, assured that the truth of any tale is everlastingly unfinished, that there are no fixed or foregone conclusions. That there remains the ineradicable hope of finding yet one more truth or one more meaning buried in the same old stories we've been living.

VI

THE WIND THUNDERED AND CAROMED AMONG THE CANYON
walls.

Guarding the entrance to the canyon were two stone pillars, like
the portal to a Philistine temple. Up and down the pillars, just beyond
the reach of my fingers, were carved moons and hooves and feathers,
talons and raindrops, symbols from a lost hieroglyphic. There was
graffiti, too, proper names in Spanish and English and words from
Indian languages amid the casual blasphemies, the star dates, and the
Maltese crosses.

The words and symbols, sacred and profane, were all mixed up, the
alphabet of an apocalypse that had come and gone. The stones, it
seemed, had been steeped in the dreams of a lunatic.

Topmost was a carving of a burrowing owl with spread wings. I
stepped back and peered: the owl clutched a brace of spikes in its
talons.

At that moment, a man dressed in a ragged cloak ran barefoot
from behind a boulder and proceeded to thrash me with a leafy
branch, belling like a hound as he did so. I covered my face with my
elbows and shouted for the man to stop.

The man stood back and lowered the branch. He reached out and
brushed my shoulder and said, "I didn't hurt you, boy."

"No. No."

"I'm the ditch boss," he said. "You gotta earn your way in. Everyone's gotta pay."

The cloak that he wore was cut from a Lincoln-green, government-issue blanket, the kind you find in barracks and Salvation Army shelters. The thing was covered in spider web, milkweed, thistle, burrs, ladybug wing-casings, as though the man who now wore it had been dragged over the desert at the tail of a ruffian's horse. It was stitched with black thread in places, blurry with dust, and had a slit in the center through which the man's head protruded. His black curly hair was sprinkled with desiccated seed and straw, but his beard was glossy and smooth as an Athenian spear-carrier's—as kempt as if he'd just posed for a vase-painter.

My fear soon subsided, because the man's eyes were quite sane and bright, even glad beneath the smooth and sun-varnished brow.

"Now clean yourself up, kid," he said. "You can't stand in the presence of Ali lookin like a hobo."

"All right," I said. "Is there water to wash with, sir?"

"There's no water up here. Use sand. Sand is clean as water."

The sand where we stood was soft and fine, and I ran handfuls down my arms, across my neck. I took off my sneakers and rubbed my feet till they were dry and soft. I washed my face with it.

The man licked his thumbs and smoothed my eyebrows, swiped my hair from my brow, grunted in disappointment, and suffered me to pass.

I followed a sandy path among long-dead trees, through the narrowing canyon, until the path ended dead, and I found myself hemmed by soaring bronze cliffs. Here and there, hundreds of feet above, thin streams of water trickled over the verges, only to vanish in gusty mists. Up near the vanishing waterfalls, ravens sported in the crosswinds, racing their own shadows across the cliff faces. Their calls, amplified by stone, boomed off the canyon walls.

In the lower middle of the canyon's terminal wall was the black navel of a cave.

"Hello?"

In answer, a ladder appeared in extension, dropped, and struck the ground at my feet.

Three burning candles marked the three walls of the cave, their lights the only relief to my day-blindness, a blindness compounded by a thin haze of woodsmoke. In the middle of the space was a man, seated at a small fire, his back turned to the cave mouth.

He said, "There's lots a brothers coming back these days. They're not alone, neither. They're bringing ghosts with em. Couples, families, crowds of people. Mothers, grandpas, aunties. Little kids, too, still wearing rice hats like they been workin all day in some Can Tho paddy. It's killin me. Lots of sisters coming, too, hurt by the men who hurt everything they meet. That's not the worst of it, neither. Now all a sudden, all these curanderas are coming outta the woodwork. Curanderos, too—how times change! Now let me ask you a question, boy. When the land is overrun by healers, is that a sign of sickness or is it a sign of health? Well? Do you speak English, kid?"

He pointed to the earth beside him. "Sit," he said.

I did. He was a large man, perhaps seven foot six, with a head like the butt-end of a railroad tie. He wore a long, wiry, black and silver beard. He frowned as he combed the beard thoughtlessly with two fingers, his black eyes fixed on the fire.

A movement from a corner betrayed a small figure crouched at the cave wall. From my seat at the fire, I watched the work. She was pecking at the stone, tapping a slender chisel with a jeweler's hammer, her thin shoulders squared to the work.

The chisel had bitten through the fire-stained crust to reveal the fresh rock. Lambent with oxygen and light, the images were animate in line and gesture. Each figure she completed joined the long file of other figures, and that file formed a living procession that moved counterclockwise around us, along each wall.

One image was of a tall man slumped in a too-small chair.

Another showed a woman poised to dive, as one at the edge of a board, or a cliff, but graceful and serene for all that.

There was a scorpion, composed in three lines, guarding a half-moon within the compass of its pincers.

A musical notation that had yet to be invented.

A woman, face-on to the chiseler, balanced on one toe.

A whiptail following her own footprints.

An empty door frame, a burning star.

A machine that moved earth.

I knew the artist for the girl who had bathed the Spaniards' horses' legs in a dream. It was the girl who watched her cliff town burn. It was the girl who died in the cold with the others, up where the wind, one night, flushed snow devils like jackrabbits from the frozen ground.

She rocked back on her ankles and beheld her creations. On the half-lit, chiseled plains of the walls, people and animals and trees partook of a livid and common life.

"A child will lead them," Ali said, "according to some religion. It aint my business no more. I'll moon away up here in my cave like some sour-assed buddha, while the shadow of the day of days creeps across the world." He fed a stick to the fire. "The trails are fading, son, you mightn't get back this time," he said. "You can stretch out along the ground there."

"I have to go back," I said, and noticed that the girl had vanished, and I was seized with the terror that I would not get away. "Molly'll worry. I gotta go back to her."

"Suit yourself. The trees are nearly all burnt up. The streams are all dried up. The shell traders, they're gone, too. They'll come back, though. That is all I know. One day I'll wake up, and there they'll be. And they'll bring the seeds of trees you never dreamed of. But I can't speed things along. They'll appear in their own time and not a moment sooner. Till then, all I have to do is keep this one place—this one godforsaken hole in a rock wall—clean. That's my role in this

life, boy, handed down to me from the years. Just keep things tidy here.
I got nothing else. That's it."

He turned his face to me. "Get a grip, kid. You think I want you up
here bothering me? Take these with you." He handed over a wooden
box, and I heard the tinking of small bottles inside. "Molly'll know
what to do with them. Now beat it."

☙

Ray Moon! Wake up. Where did this come from?

Molly held a wooden box under my nose and opened the lid.

You gotta keep these bottles packed in wool, I said. The paints stay
warm that way, Molly, and they'll run smoother. These rocks here—
they can be used to make more paint. Here's tourmaline for night
skies, here's malachite for kingfishers. When you run out, you can buy
more from the gem traders in Gallup, or you can order by mail. Flag-
staff's a good place. There's lots a rockhounds down there.

Molly picked up three stones and held them, outstretched, toward
the light of the window.

Chalk, gypsum, I said, pointing to each in turn. These are good for
faraway cliffs. Hematite'll be good for coyotes. Or jasper.

Well, Molly said, looking from me to the stones and back. We could
use some hematite coyotes, I suppose. Boy, she said, where in the world
did you get these? And who taught you the words for these stones?
Don't lie.

Ali told me, I said. The old man of the mountain.

☙

Molly ground the stones, poured water, and apportioned the egg
whites and the sawdust and the powdered cement to concoct the
paints. She fashioned brushes from squirrel hair and completed a set
of small paintings on cardboard: a purple stream meandering through
black trees toward an orange sky; a wild goose perched on a mountaintop, beating snowstorms from its wings; people walking in a desert

with their faces turned to the sky. In one picture, a speech banner proceeds from the mouth of a field mouse, reading, *What is life?*

Molly was glad to have found a solution to the eternal difficulties of drawing animals. She no longer tried to draw their muscles, she explained, but their motion. This she learned, she told me, from the paints themselves, though I did not understand what she meant.

Lately, I've taken to reading the artists' lives. Leonardo, I've learned, acquired the following skill: he taught himself to see a canvas as a pane of glass, and the painted images as imposed, so to speak, on the living world behind the easel. In other words, he taught himself to peer *into* the work.

I have tried to teach myself this skill of detaching one's vision and bringing the fixed figures on the image to life. Such a skill must be a sort of sorcery, and its possession not a little unsettling. Perspective may be nothing more than the sum of loss and gain, but it remains a trick of the eye, an illusion—a kind of miracle, I think.

I want to apply Leonardo's trick to Molly's lone surviving three-by-five painting, which I've kept tucked in the Boyda Book. This little work depicts a bird's-eye view of a quick, narrow river bordered by boulders, flowing through a desert. I hold the card up to the half-light and peer at arm's length, and the water begins to flow, and the current, for just a moment, whispers through the reeds.

*

I put the painted postcards in the satchel, and Molly and me set off.

We sat before the rows of pictures weighted with stones, but no one paused to look. After a few hours, the wind began to rise. Clouds gathered in an ink-and-steel palette.

The cruiser pulled up to the curb, and the sheriff got out.

Get in, he said. Both of you.

Molly began to gather the pictures. No, she said.

The sheriff winced at the sky. Get in. It's about to rain, Molly. I'll take you back home.

No, thank you.

Are you selling these without a permit? If so, I'll take them now. Molly, I'm not going to hurt you. I'll take you home and leave you there. Now get in. Get in, or you'll be cited and fined. Has that kid ever been to school? Does she send you to school, kid?

There aint a school for forty miles, Molly said, her voice an accusation.

That excuse won't wash with the county commissioner. Let's call him and see what he thinks. He'll probably send a man out today. Well?

He opened the rear door of the cruiser, and we climbed in.

We drove out of town but not in the direction of the mesa. The sheriff remained silent until the last trailers had fallen behind, and the empty desert closed in.

I'm worried about your safety, he said, with a glance at the side mirror. What do you know about that screwball who gives speeches on the plaza? He might be dangerous, Molly.

Molly didn't answer.

That little friend a yours, the sheriff continued, was giving a speech, if I remember, talking about a revolution, and how there's groups a rebels waiting to rise up out of the ground. Gonna fight tyranny and all that, help poor folks out and whatnot. He's out there now, spreading the word, in Amarillo, Tucson, Denver—aint it? He's what they call a revolutionary, I suppose. Gonna make the world a paradise for low-lifes.

He turned around and spoke through the mesh. Gonna change the world. That's what he said. Aint it?

He pulled over beneath an overpass and wrenched the lever into park.

My guess, the sheriff said, is that he hasn't gone anywhere at all. My guess is that he's bluffing. There aint no cells, no secret councils, no rebel army—none a that. And if I'm right, then he doesn't go where he says he goes, and he's not a menace to society after all. He's just a plain old liar. And a damn silly one, too. Now look up there, under that trestle. It's sorta dark up under there, so you gotta look real close. See that trash up in there?

It took a moment for the jumble of things to resolve into focus, and I saw a canvas bag and a mattress. A heavy coat hung from a girder. A bicycle lay on its side. And in the midst of those things was a man, seated cross-legged in the shadow. The man under the trestle, I could see, was looking down at us.

Well look who we found here, the sheriff said. If that aint the messiah himself. You two wait here.

He took his nightstick from the passenger seat, climbed out, locked us in from the outside, and started up the shallow slope of the revetment toward the man. Molly pulled the door handle and pushed, searched about for a window crank, cursed. She pounded the window glass with the palm of her hand and shouted, Larry!

But the man couldn't hear us. No one could. By now the cop was among the man's belongings, swatting at things with his stick. P.D. stood up and stepped back, feet planted, arms raised, shouting words we couldn't hear. The sheriff calmly lifted the bicycle upright and sent it skidding down the slope. He kicked two boxes after the bike, and they toppled and spilled their contents of books and cans. When the cop raised the stick at him, P.D. shielded his head with his arms. But the cop did not strike. He gave a parting kick to a small stove, which broke apart as it tumbled down the revetment. Finally, he holstered his truncheon and stepped gingerly back down the slope, through the scattered debris of P.D.'s worldly possessions.

By the time the sheriff had settled into his seat and turned the ignition, Molly had quieted and wiped her eyes.

He said, I'm sorry you had to see that, girl. But it's important to know people for what they really are. They'll always lie to you. Not me, though. I'll always tell you the truth.

He pulled onto the highway, spitting gravel.

You're gonna be my wife, Molly, and you're gonna have my children. I'll give you everything you need. You and I will be happy. You'll have nice clothes and money and a home of your own. I'll buy you a car, too, so you don't have to tramp up and down the highway like some witless slut.

He glanced over his shoulder, then, and for the first time his eyes met mine. His brow was bright with sweat, his eyes misty and satisfied. He turned back to the road and hit the gas.

You don't have to answer me now, he said. I'll give you some time to get used to it. Don't think of going anywhere. I know where you come from, I know where your family lives, and I have the wherewithal to track down a runaway field rat in this state.

He regarded himself in the mirror.

You're tired, he said. Me, too. I understand. It's been a day full of surprises.

When we returned to the sleeper, Molly did not enter but walked around and vomited in the patch of turned earth where the garden had been. When she finished, she sat at the table and laid her head on her arms. When she woke, she wiped her hair from her face, put a water bottle in the satchel, and set off.

I had the feeling she wanted to go alone, so I lay down in the back room. The sleeper door closed, and the windy-ticking quiet settled in. I felt miffed that she didn't call me along, then I felt foolish and got angry at myself, for I was old enough to know better. Then someone entered the sleeper, and the door to my room opened.

Let's take a walk, Molly said.

I closed the book, put my shoes on, and all my childish resolution vanished in an instant.

Passing through a wide expanse of cholla, we found them in bloom. I had noticed, over the previous days, the first tentative signs of the season—a few flowers opening here and there. Now the branches of every cactus were arrayed with waxy flowers. The desert had been suddenly decorated—surreptitiously in the night, so it seemed—with a hundred thousand candles the color of wine-in-water.

We paused to watch the bees, now burry with pollen, scouring the petals.

We could learn from them, Molly said.

I expected a pleasant word about the rewards of patience or the transience of beauty. But I was disappointed.

We need to protect ourselves with thorns, she said.

We arrived at the river. Thirsty, I lay down on my stomach to drink.

Molly called sharply to me. This is how we're gonna drink from now on, she said.

She crouched at the edge, dipped cupped hands to the water, and raised the water to her lips.

This way's more disciplined, Ray Moon. We're not animals. We're gonna start actin more soldierly.

Disciplined was not the way we did things. The word left a sour taste. Discipline robbed the spirit of the hour of its volition—and that spirit had guided us well enough for months. Of course, I would not have figured my little protest in this way at that time, but I clearly recall that gratifying flux of injured pride.

In truth, the rebuke rankled, and I resented it.

There was in those days a changed economy to her words and actions. She rested less, broke for water rarely, stepped more lightly. When I lingered over a horned lizard—out of stubbornness, I admit— she ignored me and turned toward the fording place.

But over time, this new purposiveness became infectious: I spoke less, kept within sight, watched my step. Checked the sky for weather.

There was no sign of people on either shore or among the over-shadowing cliffs as we stepped across the dry rocks, shoes in hand. On the flat top of a midstream stone, we sat side by side, and Molly dipped the canteen in the silver riffles.

A bird perched on a nearby ocotillo.

Molly, I said, I forgot the Boyda Book.

She glanced at the bird. That's a flycatcher, she said.

As if to demonstrate the truth of that, the bird sprung from the branch, fluttered in place, nipped a bug on the wing, and resumed its perch.

We don't need the book no more, she said. I got that book in my brain by now. Ready?

We crossed the stream and continued into the desert, walking for miles and hours toward a distant timbered ridge. Halfway to the crest, I stepped over a blackened tree. At first, I believed the tree had been struck by lightning, but then I noticed other trunks lying about pell-mell—the whole slope covered in dead black trees. A few trees stood yet, charred and shorn of branches, like maypoles from forgotten saintly days.

Molly was far ahead by now, still climbing, striding briskly over the burnt trunks.

I caught up and hurried along behind her. We reached the crest together. Grass and flowers in profusion grew from the scorched earth, in the cool strip of shade to be found on the north side of each fallen tree.

Molly sat on a black trunk and caught her breath. She picked up a stone lying at her feet and dropped it in her pocket. I sat beside her.

The burnt trees overlay the surrounding hillsides, as though the mountain had been draped with sprawling fish nets in want of mending. Several months had passed since the fires. Now new life burgeoned at every interstice, a livid greening nourished on char.

This is where your uncle died, Ray Moon.

I scanned the slope for a sign, a bit of blue flannel, the dull gleam of boot leather. I nearly expected to see a figure appear on the crest above, waving high and slow like people do at a distance. Or a figure like ourselves, seated on a nearby log, his back to us as he faced down-valley, intent on something no one else could see.

But there was nobody there. I felt Molly shudder once as she stifled her grief, and I walked away. A stone's throw from Molly, I found a file of blue flowers growing on the sunny side of a trunk. I picked two and returned and gave them to her.

Lupines, I said. See? I'm learning the names of things by heart, Molly, like you are. I think we don't need the book anymore, too.

She took them from my hand.

You're learning more than that book could ever teach you, she said. You're learning how to be a man.

When I sat beside her, she asked me if I missed my uncle, and I told her I did.

Ah, how terrible, Molly said. How terrible it must be not to have someone to take care of.

It has taken me a lifetime to understand what she meant by that.

She took a stone from her pocket and set it on the ordinary ground, and I saw that she was very lonely, and I knew that my uncle, too, was very lonely in this burnt place.

I asked Molly to tell me about my uncle. Straightaway she lifted her face, as though she'd heard a welcome cry.

She listened to the voice of memory awhile.

He comes into the diner one day, she said, the place I worked at, and he orders a coffee. He didn't order any food but sat by himself in the booth, looking out the window.

Molly turned the thought of him.

He seemed so dang miserable, Ray Moon, wearing that old jacket, she said. Engine grease on his knuckles. He looked like one a them tranjents. I learned a lot about people by waiting tables, and I could tell straight off he'd got nobody to take the time off his hands for him, so he carried all of it around with him, everywhere he went, which is a weary thing to do. It's like Judy would say—Judy was one of the girls, you know—Judy'd say, Some men got this lost look to them, like they're in it way over their heads. This is how Judy said it: some men are like cavemen who can't make fires, but they're too ashamed to admit it, so they freeze to death real quiet.

Ah, but it aint good to laugh about dying of cold, Molly continued, resting her head in the palm of one hand, looking along the cindered ground.

Then there's other cavemen, she said, who are too proud to admit that they can't make a fire. That kind's no use to me. They'll try, Ray Moon, and they might even convince themselves they built you a fire, but it aint a nice fire. Deep down, they know it, too, but they cover it up with a lot of loud talk. Or worse.

Molly, you know a lot about different kinds of men, I said.

It aint so, though. All I know about men I learned from Judy Ortega. Now that girl was smart. Molly laughed at the clouds, a loud clean laugh with life in it. I was glad to hear it.

She went on. It's that first kind, though, what cuts the sorrier figure. They live without somebody—not because they don't want to—but because they just don't have a clue. I suppose I'm a sucker for such a soul. He was a sad thing sitting there. So I give him a slice of apple pie. Then he comes in the next day, and I'll tell you what, Ray Moon, I believe he'd practiced all night long on how to thank me.

At our feet, a single paper butterfly came to light on the tip of a burnt blade of wood.

He came in the next day after, and he asked me if I was happy. He was careful like that. He talked like a person handles glass.

The sun was setting above the mountains, now doubly clothed in ash and evening.

Long sashes of clouds unraveled deep in the sky, windflaws the color of coral.

Molly reached for my hand.

Time to go, she said.

⸻

Early next morning, we took a walk as usual, and when we returned to the sleeper, Molly sat down, pale and listless, on the bottle-crate stoop. I think I'm gonna be sick, she said.

She slipped to her hands and knees as the nausea fought through her. While she vomited in the sand, she held her own hair in her fist behind her neck. But much of her hair slipped her clutch and was splattered, so I helped gather it back up, and held it there while she finished. She gasped, retched, crawled a short way, sprawled flat in the sand, thanked me for my help, and announced that she was about to die.

Solemnly, she commanded me to help her inside, where she lay for hours in a perspiring delirium, and expressed the desire to die faster. I said I'd fetch Fargo, but she ordered me to fetch paper and pencil instead, so that she might dictate, as she put it, her last willing testament.

To Ingrid she left her jacket and winter boots, and to Fargo she left everything in the sleeper, and with that, I assumed, the business was concluded. Her brow had by now acquired a cool pale sheen, and with her hands folded on her chest and her ankles together, she resembled Edward Confessor recumbent on the lid of his crypt. In this state, she pronounced my inheritance.

To you, Ray Moon, she said—and I do not know from which book or movie she had conned the protocols of passing on—To you, she said, I leave the binoculars and the Boyda Book.

⚓

That day, she took no food, slept little, and endured bouts of nausea that grew less frequent but more fearful. I roamed about and took account of those matters that would demand my attention in the event of Molly's demise.

I set a bucket beside the cot, lit the burner to heat a can of soup. Through the window I saw two figures, Ingrid and P.D., walking up the track toward the sleeper. I ran to meet them, and Ingrid took my hand.

P.D. and I looked on from the foot of the cot as Ingrid knelt and stroked Molly's hair.

I'm dying, Molly said with grave equanimity.

Ingrid smiled and placed her hand on Molly's stomach. It's much worse than that. You're pregnant.

I was down at the river, P.D. said, and I saw the spirit of God moving over the face of the desert, and I saw tongues of fire descend on this very place.

Ingrid and I looked at the ceiling, for in fact there was a trace of burning in the air.

Molly lifted her head. Ray Moon, she said. Go see that the roof's not burning.

Smells like burnt tomatoes, Ingrid said, sniffing.

I ran to turn the burner off. I'm sorry, Molly, I said. I burned the soup!

Ingrid laid her head on Molly's belly, but Molly was too nauseated to share in the amusement. P.D., she said, will you bring me that sack—the one by the wall.

He brought it to the bedside.

Open it.

He held a portable camp stove in his hand.

Molly, he said.

I thought you could use it, Molly said. Or you could give it to someone who needs it. You probably meet a lot of people, riding your bicycle all round the country.

Yes, it's true, he said quietly, holding the thing in both hands like a chalice. I do meet a lot of people. Thank you.

As P.D. cinched the sack, taking solemn care to do so, I saw that a great old age had stolen over him.

—

Molly recovered for a time and embarked on her pregnancy with little complaint and less discussion. She was attended by a series of friends—P.D., Ingrid, Fargo—who arrived at irregular intervals. Her friends were so many moons whose orbits carried them unpredictably but periodically past the sleeper door, bearing applesauce and beans and cans of Green Giant peas. Fargo brought sausage. Ingrid brought stories from the hospicio and cans of Coca-Cola and homemade bread, and she and Molly shared talk.

On her way out one evening, Ingrid bent over me and took my head between her hands and said to me, in deadly earnest, Do not let Molly see a snake, Ray Moon, hear? If you see a snake, you chase it off, hear me? Don't make any faces at Molly, neither. And if you see a spider in here, catch it and set it free outside, okay? Don't you dare kill it! Now repeat these things back to me. Go.

So I did, to the letter.

Over the coming days, she added to the list of mysterious prohibitions: no peeling potatoes or sucking on hard candy inside the trailer, no needless talking after sundown. And one day, when Ingrid unaccountably changed the salt in the saltshaker, Molly smiled and didn't ask why.

▲

As the weeks passed, our walks diminished in time and distance. Mornings, she came out of the sleeper to help me look for stones; she stood straight and directed me here and there like a French field marshal. Afternoons, as she perspired in a sleepless dream on the cot, I struck out alone to gather stones, and when I brought them home, she named them, unerringly, as lunatics and children do.

The hammered yellow heat of those days relented by touches, as the weeks passed, and the sky cooled to cornflower. At times, a gin-tinted token of juniper slipped by from some faraway cliff, like a ribbon of cool water.

And all that time, she said very little about the child she carried. She may have assumed that I didn't have a thought of my own on the matter—that I didn't know enough to speak sensibly about such things.

But I did have thoughts.

The child took its cue from its mother and held its peace in my presence.

The nights turned cool, and three cans of fuel appeared beside the sleeper one day—courtesy of Fargo—and we took to turning on the stove at night.

P.D., Ingrid said, make yourself useful. Go to Saint Alban's. It's Tuesday, the pantry's open. We need some food in this place. And blankets! Find some more blankets! These aren't enough no more.

P.D. burst out and pedaled furiously down the lane, and Ingrid paused to watch him from the window.

A strange bird, she said.

He had been gone but a short time when the sheriff's cruiser rumbled up the track. Ingrid whispered to the window a word I'd never heard.

Molly heard, and knew.

He let himself in, removed his sunglasses, ignored Ingrid and me, and stepped to Molly's bedside.

I heard you had something cookin up here, he said. You know it's mine but you didn't tell me. Now why is that? Well, never mind. I'm here now, and you're gonna have my son. Lookit you, Molly, he said, sweeping one slow hand over her. Just lookit you.

Molly didn't respond. He reached for her hand.

Please make it quick, Ingrid said, cross-armed by the window. The girl needs to rest now.

Pardon? Of course, you're right. The sheriff did not take his eyes off Molly. We'll just be a minute, he said.

He knelt and brushed her hair from her brow. Molly, I made the arrangements, he said. I'll be sending a car up to take you to your new place. I bought a house on some nice land, timber and water, on a hill just down the highway from here. Bobby made me a nice deal on it.

Can't you see you're agitating her? Ingrid said. She opened the door. You come back some other time.

The sheriff's eyes lingered a moment over Molly's averted face, then he stood and stepped in front of Ingrid, reached out, and pulled the wig from her head. The ease with which the woman's hair came away in his hand surprised him, and for a moment they stood together, suspended in a moment of disbelief.

Her skin shone in the sunlight, and the light gathered in a single point at the very crown of her head. She did not flinch, but stood eye to eye with him. She held out her hand, then, and he returned the wig uncompelled.

She did not replace the wig, but held it in her hands.

The fear that the man had brought into the sleeper—the fear that had mantled the two women and me—dissolved in that instant, and was replaced by another spirit, one of a wholly different order. And in the presence of that other spirit, Ingrid sized the man from head to toe.

You're an ugly human being, she stated.

But he was not one to loosen his clutch on authority. Authority was what he possessed in this world.

That's funny words coming from a sick old witch, he said, and paused at the door. Start packing, Molly. My man'll be by in a few days to get you.

I met P.D. as he was walking his bike up the track. I told him that the sheriff had come to the trailer and that he was cruel to Ingrid. I told him how that sheriff was going to send a man to get Molly.

P.D. considered the words as he pushed the bicycle up the hill.

A solitary cyclone of dust whirled, far across the desert, tracing the hem of a mountain.

Why did Molly get pregnant now, P.D.? I asked. She don't have any money. Maybe it'd been better to wait.

Look, boy, he said. The revolution is coming, and the children of the revolution are neither male nor female, but soldiers, and they neither marry nor are given in marriage. The seeds of new life and new beginnings are nourished by the showers of destruction. No one's gonna take Molly, or the child. Not that man, not nobody. I can promise you that, young Ray. Everything's gonna be fine. Believe it.

The sheriff did in fact send a man, and though the man was a bully, he lost his nerve in Ingrid's presence, and he conceded to Molly's claims of illness, for in fact she was pale and thin. But these rebuffs bought only a little time, and they all knew it.

Molly began to gnaw her nails beside the window; she got irritable with me now and then. She borrowed against luck to buy time. In every person's life—if they live long enough—there comes a moment when one finds oneself overtaken by events. Then, the nauseating sensation of being trapped begins to nibble away in the stomach, and you know that the time has come. The creditors of fortune gather like eagles on the roof, your feet become feet of clay, and you realize there is no escape.

Molly began to scare at noises.

One morning, I woke to an empty place.

⬧

I went to town and did not see her at Saint Alban's, nor at the fountain. I went to the mayor's office and saw the sheriff's car parked in front, as it usually was. I went to the post office, and the clerk told me a woman who looked like Molly had been there and gone. I turned these things over in my mind as I walked, finding no solution to my thoughts, till I found myself at the edge of the river. The coracle was missing.

I set off downstream, along the shore. How different the land looked to me now, on foot and alone. The sunstruck cliffs receded, and the cairns, whose mysterious significance had invited our common wonder, had become as the tombs of strangers. What had once been revealed in Molly's company, was now concealed, deceiving. The caves of Zuni holy women became the lurking places of thieves, or worse, and every canyon drew away into a wilderness of ostriches and jackals. After a long hike, I came once more to the lava fields and saw the coracle dragged carelessly to shore, half in-and-out of the water. I covered the craft with brush and set off.

Snowflakes tumbled like mayflies in the sudden cold. Blue clouds settled on the far peaks, snuffing the sunlit crags.

When I got to the cave, I found Molly asleep on her back, her hands folded on her belly. Near her, a small fire had been kindled. The fire was dead now, a patch of cold cinders and scorched fragments of paper: the powder blue stationary of her brother's letters, and the white stock of her painted postcards.

I knelt beside her and placed my hand on her hand.

"Ah, Ray Moon," she said, but did not open her eyes. "I saw you coming from far away. I saw you walking along the river, crossing the volcano fields. Lay down and rest now, boy."

I lay facing the mouth of the cave, where the snowflakes fell. She covered me with a corner of her jacket. I said, "Molly, why did you burn your brother's letters? You got bad news, I think."

"You're very smart, Ray Moon," she said. "I got a telegram from my father. He lives in Barstow. Tommy died just a few days ago. He died far away from here."

"But why did you burn the letters?"

"I can't read them, and I can't throw them away. So I burned them. Do you understand?"

"Yes."

"You're thin, boy. Are you hungry?"

"No. Are you hungry, Molly?"

"No."

"Why did you burn the paintings?"

"Do you want to go with me, Ray Moon? I have a plan."

A sparrow alighted with a brief puff of dust at the cave entrance.

"To where, Molly?"

"This river goes all the way to a city. We'll take it there. I'll get a job. You can go to a school."

"Why won't we take a bus or hitch a ride?"

"On the river, you see, we'll leave no tracks. Then he won't find us."

"That's smart, Molly."

"I know. I been thinkin in here. Of a lot of things."

I fell asleep there for a few minutes—perhaps an hour—maybe days. When I opened my eyes, the shadows of evening leaned in at the cave mouth. I woke Molly and helped her to sit up, for she was in pain from the hike across the lava fields, and now we had to recross them, and that was only the beginning. As we set off, I walked ahead, spying the least onerous path over the stones.

When we reached the riverside, I strapped the coracle to my shoulders. We turned upstream and made our way by the sandy path that threaded the boulders. The mesas receded, in wide sweeping steps, back to the skyline.

As we walked, darkness filled the draws and the canyons.

Night fell swiftly and caught us miles from home. As there was no moon, there was no question of continuing to pick our way along the riverside trail or crossing the desert to the highway. So I gathered logs from the shore, bone-white wood bleached by wind and water. The bigger logs I propped against a boulder as a windbreak, and piled the smaller ones for a fire, which I kindled from the matches I found in Molly's satchel. We had no food but drank a little from the river.

The Milky Way appeared like a river of sands, low and parallel to the skyline, rolling overhead as the heavens turned. We shivered and made names for the things we saw up there, until the sky was fairly crowded with appliances and waterfowl, demons, and gewgaws.

"There's the Tea Cup," Molly said. "Look there, Ray Moon. There's the Centipede."

We found the Great Salmon and the Tricycle, the Monkey Skull and the Shiny Fern, and many other things that had long been buried in time. At every new discovery, each of us saw what the other had seen, which is a wonderful sort of game.

Very late, when the night was stacked to the rafters with the eternal counterpart of every mortal thing, we even found the Devil's Cow, which, as everyone knows, had not been seen for a very long time.

I put the final sticks on the fire, and we slept, side by side, fitfully.

In the freezing predawn Molly woke me. She was very unwell by then, and shivering. After a few hours' hike, footsore and hungry, we arrived back at Santa Juana de Arco just as the sun crowned the eastern cliffs.

In the plaza, beneath the old cottonwood, a small crowd had gathered, some in slippers, some in bedclothes, some wrapped in particolored blankets. Their faces were turned toward the higher branches of the tree. One man held his hand over his mouth. One woman held her brow in her palm.

Because we approached from the far side, we did not at first see the object of their attention. When we came around and joined the crowd, we saw a ladder set against the trunk, a tall ladder reaching into the shadows of the branches, and a man climbing the rungs with a coil of rope around his shoulder.

Higher up in the branches was another man, suspended by the neck. Like a monstrous fruit, he hung heavily there among the golden leaves. His face was turned down and away, as though bending its bloated gaze on the crowd. The man was in uniform, the silver piping plainly visible along the seams of his trousers. The revolver in its well-oiled holster weighed at his hip like an anchor stone. Molly took my hand and turned away.

By the time we arrived at the sleeper, it was full day. Ingrid waited there, shaking her head. Where were you at, Molly? I was looking all over town for you. Oh, you're cold.

She wrapped an arm around Molly's shoulder and led her to the door.

You two, she said. Where have you two been all this time?

Ingrid!

I know, child, she said, pressing my head to her hip with her free hand. Now get inside. I have a hot meal and blankets for you.

Warm weather returned with a round of late-season fires, abetted by the autumn dry spell.

All day the little mismatched convoys of pickups sped back-and-forth along the highway, and we could see, even at a distance, the truck beds bearing crews of men wearing blue and red and yellow helmets, all abristle with shovels and axes. Molly sat in the lawn chair, her fingers laced beneath her belly, watching not speaking.

The winds veered to every point of the compass. Now and then, the smell of fires gusted across the mesa, and sometimes a flake of ash tumbled past like a moth. Smoke gathered in clouds, the clouds trickled rained, and the rain darkened the land.

The sun appeared passingly in its phases—glossy and dim, copper and nickel—its magnitude as changeable as the wind.

And in the midst of the smoke and clouds—with the unsayable timeliness of things—the sun eclipsed.

. The day had dimmed by degrees throughout the morning, and at noon the smoke parted to reveal a sun now flat and cold and half-devoured by shadow. The winds went to ground with the vanishing of the light, and the land turned inward, as flowers do at evening, and all things found, for a time, their quietus. Even the fires, it seemed, held their tongues.

In the fullness of the eclipse shadow, Molly and I sat in our chairs in the dust, wondering at the incandescent dark that had risen out of the earth.

During eclipses, so I've read, the early peoples gathered in the open to shout and throw stones and beat gongs and to blow their reed flutes at the sky, in hopes of chasing off the demon who was swallowing the master of light. And knowing, as people have always known, that this trouble would pass with time, their victory over the powers of darkness was followed by wild ceremonies of gratitude.

If we had known then of the old rituals, perhaps we would have beat our scorched pots and pans with sticks and spoons, shouted bad words at the sky, called the demon by his very name. But we didn't know about those things.

The lines of faraway fires stood forth more brightly in the gloom. I imagined the weary men scattered across those mountainsides, a long thin rank with blackened faces and blackened hands. I wondered how the eclipse transpired, way up there among the firemen.

Some whispered suggestion, I imagine, came to each of them as, one by one, they paused in their work and straightened their aching backs, overtaken by the strangeness. Perhaps, one of those men pushed the stained helmet from his brow, and another leaned on his fire rake as on a crutch, and another grimaced at the sky, as they sought within themselves, or in the faces of their companions, some answer to the untimely shadow.

The day after someone hanged the sheriff, a patrol car came up the lane from the highway. Molly was too weak to stand, so I let the young officer inside. The man sat at the table, took his cap off, and shared a few sober observations about the fires. Molly told me to boil water.

No need to make coffee, young man, he said. I won't be here long enough to drink it. You might know why I'm here, ma'am, since the whole town knows. I'm sorry to ask, but is the baby his?

I don't know, Molly said.

Do you know anyone who might've wanted to do harm to him?

Harm? Sure. Lots a folks, I'd bet. He was mean.

We figured it needed two or three strong men, the officer said, to hoist a body that high up in a tree.

Yes.

There's one man in state custody, he said. But one man didn't hoist that fellow up by himself. Well, that sheriff must've done something.

I believe he said this as a gentle sort of jest, but Molly didn't answer to it. She asked, What's his name?

I don't recall. A vagrant, I think.

The man glanced at me. Is the kid yours and his?

No. Just mine.

He doesn't look like you.

He don't need to.

You're right about that. That wasn't called for. I apologize, ma'am.

He thanked Molly, rose from the chair, and said to me, Let's take a walk to the cruiser, kid. I'll let you work the flashers.

He rested his hand on my shoulder as we crossed the empty sunlight to the vehicle. He wasn't dressed in a charcoal and gunmetal uniform like the sheriff. No shined boots on his feet, but a pair of scuffed low-quarters. No silver piping down the seam of his pants. No polished buckle, no chevron on his shoulder. His hair covered his ears, and he was carelessly shaved. ARAGUZ was stamped on his crooked silver name badge. From the waist up, he might have been the postman.

What's the good word, kid? Any funny stories you want to tell me?

Was the sheriff a friend of yours? I asked.

Officer Araguz paused at the driver door and glanced at me. A look of curious amusement crossed his face.

No, he said. From what I've heard of him, I'm glad to say I didn't know that man from Adam. But thanks for asking, young man. That was nice of you to think that way. You're a good son. You take care of your mama, all right?

He drove off.

That night, the stove rumbled like a gorged lion. I stepped out into the cold and stood beneath the sky now stippled and daubed with clouds of stars.

The sky reveals its true self in the small hours, and only a few sad or sleepless or shady people will ever know how starlight does burn brighter than daylight, if one stands up straight, alone in the dark, and listens.

A star arced across the sky, and its passage was attended by a sound like silk being torn in two. But that was only my imagination.

I stood in the shadow of the sleeper, beyond the skirt of light from the window. A vehicle came up the track. Ingrid emerged from the car, in the company of a nurse from the hospicio, and together they entered the sleeper.

When I entered, after a few hours, Molly lay back, pale and perspiring, eyes closed. Ingrid had placed the linen bundle on Molly's stomach and guided her hands to the child. Molly knew the bundle for what it was, and her lips parted, but she did not speak.

Ingrid tucked a damp ribbon of hair behind her ear.

When her color changed, the nurse peered beneath the blanket. Quickly, Ingrid took the child and placed it with a word in my arms, and the two women carried Molly out to the truck. Within a single hectic moment the sleeper was empty. An engine roared alive, gravel splattered against the sleeper, headlights swept across the wall. The car stormed off, and I was alone.

But not alone.

A small sound informed me I was holding the baby too tight.

I parted the linen and saw, for the first time, the small grave patient face. She seemed to be waiting for me to account for myself. I had nothing to say, but the child did not hold this against me.

We shared a moment of mutual and unself-conscious scrutiny, on terms admissible to us both, neither granting nor conceding anything, sunk in a study of the other's life, which may have been, for all I knew, nothing more than a mirror reflection of one's own.

Her eyes were the color of slate in rain. She looked at me, without fear or demand, but with an unadorned interest in this creature—that is, myself—whom she might just as well pity as befriend. On my part, I was surprised that the child was not blind like a kitten, but was born wholly aware. With her, there was as yet none of the unease or suspicion we learn to feel in unfamiliar places. She merely exhibited, untaught, the timeless courtesies of the visitor, who expected nothing, appreciated the small efforts made on her behalf, but who nevertheless would soon be on her way again—thanks and farewell!—refusing to detain us longer than was absolutely necessary, and unwilling, at any cost, to impose on our hospitality.

All this, of course, I imagined later. In truth, during the time I held the child, she never moved, never made a sound, and never opened her eyes.

Ingrid appeared before me, said something I didn't understand, and reached for the bundle.

I didn't let go.

She spoke again, sharply this time, and took the child.

It was then I saw the empty cot, the turned blankets, and the blood. The open door swung lazily on its hinges, and the cold air entered with the scents of winter stars, and the smoke of faraway fires.

⬥

All that night and all the next day I waited, but no one returned. Engine trucks and pickups barreled up and down the highway, on their way to the fires.

After sundown, I headed out to search for Ingrid or Molly, taking the direct way down the slope of the mesa toward town. Files of cars lined both sides of the highway, and the town blazed with lights, for Santa Juana was deep in the annual celebration of the saint for which the town was named, for whom several days of revelry were set aside.

Barrel fires blazed. Torches and festival lamps illuminated the drifting clouds of dust that loomed in technicolor above the town. A convoy of cars and pickups—with clutches of howling children in the beds—crawled through the parti-colored haze.

Knots of people greeted each other with raised bottles, as though every last citizen was, for just this one day of their lives, right on time.

A solitary drunken specter in a white shirt lurched across the street, breasting headlight beams with his arms raised.

I passed three women standing over a body facedown on the pavement. Whether they were laughing or weeping, I didn't know.

Where you going, kid?

A shadow in a wide brim hat confronted me, a figure backlit by noise and fire.

Fargo!

I been looking for you, he said. These godawful people. Let's go.

The tumult faded as we made our way out of town to Fargo's truck, parked in the dark a short walk away.

The boys in blue were around this evening, asking questions, Fargo said as he drove toward the mesa. You'll stay at my place now, young Ray. Don't worry, I won't make you go to school. George Washington, Christopher Columbus. God-knows-what nonsense they teach these days. What do you say, boy? I'll teach you the fine points of four stroke engine repair. If you're smarter than me, you'll make enough money to buy this miserable town.

Where's Molly? I asked.

〜

Where's Molly.

I saw Molly again, or think I did.

I was driving a bus, a job I held for many years. It was a good job, with good pay and benefits. I liked it and I did it well. You spend all day out on your route, nobody looking over your shoulder. You meet people.

There were regulars who boarded at the same time from the same stop for years. Of course, I gave them names. The woman who leaped up the steps with a cheery greeting, in defiance of her many years, was Lambspring.

The man who offered unsolicited and oath-edged lectures to the passengers about city corruption was Hammurabi, for he was well schooled in the law.

And the man who one day boarded with a pigeon feather stuck to his loafer has done penance ever since, for he was christened Pennyfeather. Someday soon, before I retire—when I'm feeling sufficiently querulous—I'll reveal his hidden identity to him. By the looks of him, he won't be happy about it.

I recall the weather of that day. The air was saturated—sticky, heavy. When she boarded, she sat directly behind the driver's partition. I did not have a good view of her, but only the reflection of her reflection in the mirror at the rear of the coach. I noticed how she turned to the window glass, in posture very like a woman who sat beside a window in a trailer atop a mesa in New Mexico fifty years before.

No one paid her any mind, of course. But then, a boy seated across the aisle climbed onto his seat, stood straight up, faced the woman, and stared wide-eyed at her.

His actions startled his mother. She did not at first scold the boy, but sat gazing up at him, caught in a moment of astonishment at how tall, how grave her child had suddenly become.

When I pulled over to collect the zone fares, the seat where the woman had sat was empty.

🔊

Where's Molly? I asked Fargo, as he steered the truck up the track.

He didn't answer at first.

Let's get some rest now, he said. We'll look tomorrow. The evil of the day is sufficient thereof.

I told Fargo I meant to get some clothes before I went on to his place, and I climbed down at the door of the sleeper. Inside, I filled a canteen with water, placed two potatoes and a box of matches in the satchel, strapped the coracle on, and set off into the dark.

When I reached the river, I found Molly's punting pole where she'd left it. I pushed the boat into the stream, climbed in, stowed the satchel, and shoved off.

The land opened beneath the stars, the boulders sank behind me, the water flowed smooth and wide.

The sun rose as the hills revolved. Small birds arrived to tap the surface.

Mountains came down to the river to drink.

On the eastern bank appeared a field, and three women standing there. They leaned on their hoes and watched as I passed. One woman waved. Another cupped her hands to her mouth to call to me, but I could not understand the words, she was too far away. I did not wave, though I wanted to.

There's a story I once read, and in the story, it is said that people, after they depart, return as clouds to visit us on quiet days, down here in our earthbound work and life. Because of this, the living must remember, every morning, to turn their faces to the skies so the clouds might recognize their own, might gaze a moment on their loved ones before a dry wind carries them away.

AUTHOR'S NOTES

There are moments in *Molly*, such as a reference to a place of emergence and to a mask, that draw from the myths and traditions of Native Americans—namely Hopi, Zuni, Pueblo, and Navajo—insofar as these are known in English translation. The presence of these references in this work of fiction seemed necessary to the setting; any depiction of New Mexico would be, I believe, incomplete without them.

THANKS

With sincere gratitude to Mike Good, editor at Autumn House Press, for his generosity and patience, his unfailing good sense, and his excellent editorial advice. This book would be much poorer without his assistance.

ABOUT THE AUTHOR

Kevin Honold was born in Cincinnati, Ohio, and is currently a history and special education teacher in Santa Fe, New Mexico. He is the author of the poetry collection, *Men as Trees Walking* (Ohio State University Press, 2010), and most recently an essay collection, *The Rock Cycle* (University of New Mexico Press, 2021), which won the *River Teeth* Nonfiction Prize in 2020. *Molly* is his first novel.

American Home by Sean Cho A.

WINNER OF THE 2020 AUTUMN HOUSE CHAPBOOK PRIZE, SELECTED BY DANUSHA LAMÉRIS

Under the Broom Tree by Natalie Homer

The Animal Indoors by Carly Inghram

WINNER OF THE 2020 CAAPP BOOK PRIZE, SELECTED BY TERRANCE HAYES

speculation, n. by Shayla Lawz

WINNER OF THE 2020 AUTUMN HOUSE POETRY PRIZE, SELECTED BY ILYA KAMINSKY

All Who Belong May Enter by Nicholas Ward

WINNER OF THE 2020 AUTUMN HOUSE NONFICTION PRIZE, SELECTED BY JAQUIRA DÍAZ

The Gardens of Our Childhoods by John Belk

WINNER OF THE 2021 RISING WRITER PRIZE IN POETRY, SELECTED BY MATTHEW DICKMAN

Myth of Pterygium by Diego Gerard Morrison

WINNER OF THE 2021 RISING WRITER PRIZE IN FICTION, SELECTED BY MARYSE MEIJER

Out of Order by Alexis Sears

WINNER OF THE 2021 DONALD JUSTICE POETRY PRIZE, SELECTED BY QUINCY R. LEHR

Queer Nature: A Poetry Anthology edited by Michael Walsh

For our full catalog please visit: http://www.autumnhouse.org